5 Star Publications
3325 Donnell Drive
Forestville, MD 20747

Copyright 2009 by 5 Star Publications

ISBN-13: 978-0-9843881-3-4
ISBN-10: 0-9843881-3-3

Library of Congress Control Number: 2010900132

First Printing: December 2009

Printed in the United States

Dedication

I dedicate this book to my Great Grandparents who created the foundation from which I thrive, and my Grandfather who showed me early how to standout from the crowd. I also dedicate this work of art to my two brothers who passed away in a senseless act of violence, and my loved ones who have passed away "You live through me forever..."

Acknowledgments

First I want to thank God for allowing me to complete another journey in my life and adding another talent to my resume. I also want to thank everyone who took the time out to purchase this novel. I hope it lives up to it!!! I want to thank my mom, my little prince, little princess, the misses, and the rest of my family for sticking behind me through my days of hibernation. I also want to thank my managers for pushing me to think outside of the box and believing that I'm far from one dimensional and when others say I couldn't they say I could. A special thanks to Muhammad, Tri-E Entertainment and my DeMarco Solar family for keeping me at my best at all times. I would also like to thank DJ Dirty Rico, CFE, DJ Big John, In Style, and for those I missed, THANK YOU!!!

PUBLICATIONS PRESENTS...

4 PLAY

Never Say Never

A.J. Williams

Chapter 1

The sweet scent of Japanese Cherry Blossom oil from Bath and Body Works tickled my senses as R.Kelly's "12 play" played in the background. I'm singing every word in a mellow tone, "My mind is telling me noooo, but my body, my body's telling me yeah." I hear someone whisper shhhhhhh! My body begins to tingle from the preheated Wet Intimo Aromatherapy Massage Oil that is being poured all over me by a caramel complexion young lady with some pretty ass toes that are adorned with what I have heard called a French Pedicure. Her legs were slightly hairy with very fine light hair that only added to her sex appeal; just the sight of her will make your gun go off.

I feel a mixture of whipped cream and saliva dripping down the shaft of my manhood. All of this erotic pleasure coming from the warm mouth of a red bone with a short Rihanna hair cut. She has soft abundant 36 DDs begging for my attention. They melted in my mouth as soon as I got to them. Her lips were full and luscious. They looked as though she can suck ice cubes through a straw. She opened her mouth widely to let my penis wrestle with her tonsils. She moaned and slurped loudly trying to make more noise than Pocahontas who was determined to have her sexual screams heard. Pocahontas is an Indian type of female with some nice bright white teeth, wide hips, and voluptuous thighs. Her body had me mesmerized as I watched her hair brush gently back and forth across her ass. She's playing with herself and licking every toe on my left foot making me feel and scream like a cold skirt. Jockeying for her chance to please me was an athletic, flexible, seductive, and pretty Dove chocolate chica Bonita with all the right curves. She's taking turns with my caramel sundae chick in a quest to see who can make me cum the fastest. Just the silhouette of my chica Bonita would have your pulsing ego at attention. Her ass is poking out like a pregnant chick before the landing; with a lovely gap a tour bus can drive through.

Neither of them knows about my Jedi mind trick; as long as I keep singing, I can hold back this nut until my next birthday. It's my plan to have their jaws hurting. I'm not giving in until somebody has lockjaw. My plan quickly changed when Pocahontas crawled up onto my face and made me pull out my tongue tricks. My tongue traveled up and down her throbbing lips while sucking her clit. She screamed in ecstasy so loudly that I know the new neighbor upstairs can hear every word clearly. Now they know my government name, nickname, pet name, and some mo' shit. Just as I began to regain control of the situation, Bonita climbed on my lap, taking advantage of the fact that my dick was at full attention. She began to suck on Pocahontas' breast. The pleasure made her grind heavily onto my waiting tongue. Damn, I should've set up the camcorder! Shit! The red bone hummed as she licked my balls and rubbed her breast against my thighs. Damn! I'm sweating bullets. Bonita screamed, "Papi, I'm cumming". She is having the orgasm of her life from riding my dick like a professional bull rider. "Oh, yes Daddy!" Pocahontas screams before her body exploded leaving my face looking like a glazed Dunkin Donut. All four women were looking at each other, feenin' to taste one another's juices. They began to seduce each other. I'm sitting here feeling like a King watching them play naked Twister for me! I have achieved every man's dream; four sexy, freaky, and fine ass women screaming my name at once, in unison, and like a professional gospel choir.

I close my eyes and try to take it all in. The feeling of cold steel makes me open them to see that they have brought out the handcuffs and blind folds. It's about to get heated! We're back in business! Our bodies are dripping with sweat. The moaning sounds are growing louder. My finger is in somebody's ass, somebody else's pussy is getting eaten, and my dick is being jerked off at the same time. I can feel the explosion of a lifetime coming. As soon as I'm about to finally let the firecracker go off, I hear a sound that doesn't sound like it coincided with sex. It's the sound of a gun being cocked. When my blind fold is lifted up, I'm staring straight down the barrel of a pistol. The gun is pointed right between my eyes. My eyes are crossed like a special ed student. I'm using mental telepathy trying to convince the bullet not to release. Some words were whispered. I can't understand them but I know they mean that I can kiss my ass goodbye. BOOM! A shot is fired. Oh shit, am I dead? I feel something wet. I jumped up sweating bullets thinking I was bleeding or had peed in the bed. Luckily, it was neither.

I canvassed the room with my eyes to make sure it was just a dream. Scooting down to the edge of the bed I buried my face in my hands. As I'm thanking God that it was just dream, the strangest thing occurred, my alarm clock radio came on blasting…"12 Play." Are you serious? I burst out laughing.

I replayed the orgy again in my mind as I walked into my bathroom. I thought for a second how glad I am that I chose to get these custom designed heated floors so my feet wouldn't be cold. I turned on my shower, grabbed my wash cloth, and my Irish Springs body wash so I could lather up real good. When I was done massaging those mountain fresh suds into my delicate skin, I stepped out of the shower smelling like the Forbes List. Rich! Just then, my buzzer was ringing from the front door letting me know I had a guest awaiting me in the lobby downstairs. I threw on my Versace robe and slippers before hitting the intercom button.

"Who is it?" I asked

"It's your wife baby!" The voice on the other end replied

I already know who that voice belonged to, so I buzzed her on in. Who comes walking through the door? Here for a house call is my own private doctor, Dr. Meka Thomas. Part time doctor, full time freak! But, don't get it twisted; she's only that way for me. Although, I'm not really into dark skinned women, she's the exception. She has the smoothest chocolate skin you've ever seen. She reminds me of the girl Kish from the movie "Belly." This woman is fine as hell. We always have a good time when we're together and the sex is ridiculous. The only thing about her that blows me from time to time is she's always asking me if I love her. I took a vow that I will never fall in love, so I always skip over the question. She always fires right back at me with the same ole' shit.

"If you don't love me why did you tell me to get this damn tattoo? Why am I walking around with your name on my ass but you can't even tell me you love me?"

My response is always like clockwork, a simple head nod and a shoulder shrug. No words! Anything I say will piss her off and force me into a discussion I refuse to have, so I don't say shit. I just look at her. I didn't tell her to get that tattoo. No, I didn't stop her either. Matter of fact, I didn't even know she was getting it. She just popped up over my house one day with it. I must admit, my name does look good on that soft round chocolate ass of hers but that was her choice. She thought it would make her a front runner. She knows that this is a competition and she wants to win.

Meka began making breakfast as I got dressed. She prepared toast, turkey bacon, scrambled eggs, and grits; you know that Jill Scott type of shit. I always let Meka do her thing in my kitchen because she can throw down. I picked out my black DeMarco Solar Studio Collection suit with the three inch break cuff links, shining like pancake 23 on Little Richard. You know I shut shit down when I come around. I have to be on my A game when defending my clients. It's no secret that I am one of the most sought after lawyers of my time and generation. Everyone who's anyone in D.C. knows that I am the lawyer they need.

Heading to the kitchen to receive my morning greetings from Meka, I was interrupted by a text from Nikki. Nikki is a high school grade school teacher. I call her my Cherokee princess. She's sexy as hell with natural hair that drags her waistline. Her mother AND father are Indian so she is certified baby making material.

The text reads: *I am on my way to work just wanted to let you know you were on my mind. Lunch this afternoon?*

I replied: *If my schedule isn't too hectic, we sure can!*

Nikki texted back: *I love you and hopefully I will see you later.*

You already know what I 'm sitting here thinking, here goes another one with this love shit! I began shaking my head in frustration and continued digging into my home cooked meal.

"Are you ok?" Meka asked

"Yeah I'm good." I replied

When I finally took a breath from stuffing my face, I noticed Meka has disappeared. She probably went into the back for something. I'm one lucky man! I quickly figured it out that she crawled under the table when she began to give me brain surgery until my eyes rolled to the back of my head. I damn near fell out of the chair. Meka alternated her tempo between fast and slow. She was even doing some new hand tricks while sucking like a vacuum cleaner. She has been practicing. And, you know what they say, practice makes perfect! She had me busting off like a bottle rocket and like a veteran she caught every drop. Then she got up, kissed me on the neck, and walked toward the front door.

"Have a nice day baby". She whispered with a smirk on her face.

She walked off and left me in the chair on stuck, meat hanging, and mouth open. After a few minutes the blood finally returns to my legs and I can walk. So I gather myself and go wash off. Got to keep it fresh! You never know what else might pop off before the day is done. I walk to my elevator reminiscing on my morning treat. When the elevator arrives I step in and I'm greeted by the presence of the new tenant in my building. She's in the unit that's directly over top of me. I heard her moving in but this is the first time I've seen her. And boy is she something to see! She is stacked! I mean curves like a sprite bottle. Pretty skin tone. Good length of hair or weave, it's too early to tell. She has this sexy ass piercing in the corner of her top lip; I know that shit had to hurt. I can tell she got a lil' hood in her with that snake tattoo in the small of her back. Babygirl, is looking real appetizing. She must be on the way to the building gym because she's wearing her workout gear. Me being the fly gent that I am, I spoke.

"Good Morning, Miss Lady how are you?"

"I'm fine… how are you?" she replied

I extended my hand to shake hers and she did the same. This woman is fine as hell, I thought to myself.

"My name is Felix… and yours?"

"Hi Felix…I'm Toya."

"It's nice to meet you."

"Same here…it's nice to meet you as well."

By now the elevator has stopped in the lobby area. The first person we see is my favorite door man, white boy Timmy. He said he didn't take this job for the money. He took it because he gets to watch beautiful black women all day. He knows damn well this building is full of white women so when he does get to see a black woman he goes crazy. In his best attempt at sounding black Timmy yells out,

"What's up fly guy… ready to rock the courtroom?"

In my mind I'm thinking, this fool swears he's a brother. I chuckle to myself.

"What's up Timmy…I see you doing your thang." I said trying to egg him on.

"You know man… same shit…different roll of toilet paper…I see you already pushing up on the cutie in 402?"

"Naw man, we just rode the elevator together."

"Yeah right!"

"What's the deal…? I know you know!"

He starts telling me about my new upstairs neighbor. He knows everybody business or at least he thinks he does. Without taking a breath he tells me that she's a pole dance instructor during the day and a stripper by night. I stop him and make him repeat himself so I can be sure I heard him correctly.

"She's a what?"

"You heard me…she's a stripper and her stage name is Fantasy."

I nodded my head in agreement. She's damn sure a fantasy of mines. She got to be making some good money living up in here.

"She got a sugar daddy?"

"Hell yeah… if I wasn't so broke I'd be her sugar daddy."

"Man, you crazy."

"Naw for real though… she had this client, some old ass geriatric patient that was loaded and in love with her."

"You bullshittin' me?"

"Naw, real talk… This motherfucker went to see her dance for like a year. Then one night she gave him a lap dance, he went home and died. With a hard on and a smile! But peep this shit, in the will he left more for her than his kids. She got to do something right with that big ol' ass."

I laugh before asking a few more questions. Babygirl has definitely caught my eye. Believe me when I tell you that everything Felix wants Felix gets! Right now, I want her!

"Timmy… do you see any male friends come in and out of here for her?"

"If you mean is she fucking her customers…so far as I can see the answer is no. She hasn't been bringing her work home. She dances more for fun now since she has enough money to live off for 3 generations. That ass made her a millionaire…and I do mean that literally," Timmy said dying laughing.

I give my favorite white boy five and say see you later my nigga. He almost slips up and says it back. Not a complete fool he asks for permission like he always does.

"C'mon bro… give a playa a pass…you know I won't mean it like that."

"The only pass you can get from me is a bus pass. You can slip up if you want to see a real angry 100% nigga!"

He gets scared, apologizes for asking and goes off to do some work. I live downtown so there's no need to drive to work so I hop in a cab. There's never anywhere to park so I don't even bother. I spent the whole cab ride thinking about Miss Toya; she's' every woman's nightmare and every man's fantasy. The freak in me has me sitting here drifting on a melody picturing fucking her on the roof top of our building in the rain. I can see me bending her over the railing, enjoying the sites, and looking down at people that can't see us. The thrill of possibly being caught only added to the ecstasy. Well here I am. The cab ride was over now, no more fantasy it's time for the corporate reality.

As soon as I enter the office my receptionist greets me with 15 messages. 14 of them I will call later, but one is from my mother so I called her immediately.

"How's my favorite girl?"

"I'd be much better if I had some grandchildren to love. When are you going to settle down with a nice young lady instead of whoring around?"

"C'mon now mom… why you so hard on a brother?" I laughed agitating her further.

I'm sitting here getting chewed out because in my mind, I'm not ready for love or the whole family thing yet. It's too much good pussy out here.

"You're going to meet that one special lady that's going to whip it on your ass and you not going to know your ass from a hole in the ground. You're not going to have a choice but to fall for her. Watch what I tell you."

I had to cut that conversation short by using the excuse that I was late for court. No grown ass man wants to hear their mother talk about somebody turning them out.

"I love you Ma... I will call you later got to get to work.

Chapter 2

I began going over my paper work for the day. I can see that this going to be a busy day. It's so much damn paper on my desk; I can't even see the wall. This is the shit you have to go through to make partner. My secretary buzzed in on my phone letting me know that I have a meeting in the conference room with the senior partner to discuss a case with a new client. It's a married couple that is going thru a nasty divorce. These are the toughest types of cases, trying to see who deserves what. I grab the Anderson vs. Anderson file and make my way to the board room. Damn! As soon as I walk in I see a sexy ass thick lady dressed as sharp as a tack in a gray business suit. A gray suit has never looked so good! She's got to be about a size 16 plus with a short haircut. I have never dated a thick woman but this one here, she can get it! She just looks so soft and cushiony. I have all types of thoughts running through my brain about what position would be best and how I would sex her. A brother been hitting the gym but it ain't no way in hell I can pick her big ass up. I bet she can cook a nigga a meal to write home about though. I better pull myself together. Stay focused Felix, stay focused.

"Good morning Mrs. Anderson, my name is Felix and I will be assisting you with your case"

"Good morning Felix... thank you for meeting with me this morning...

I walk over and pull out the chair for her to have a seat.

...thank you." She said winking her eye at me.

My boss whispers to me to stop that flirting shit. He says this is business and she's a paying client. So I settle down and get my shit together. The meeting is running quite smoothly, we are about to wrap it up for lunch.

"Stan, I'm going to The Steak House and pick up something... do you want any?"

"No...wife got me watching the cholesterol"

I begin to laugh and he raises eyebrows like what's so damn funny. I play it off like I was laughing at something else; I ain't trying to blow my partnership opportunity over a fat joke. The room got real silent real fast. Out of nowhere Mrs. Anderson asks can she accompany me to lunch. Now what am I supposed to do? Am I to tell a paying client no? I look at my boss and he gives me the yes nod. The expression on his face is clearly saying, don't fuck this up.

We make our way outside and walk like a block and a half down the street. We go in the restaurant and are seated pretty quickly. Her phone rings. She answers and begins to give a complete run down of me to the person on the other end. I don't know how I feel about this shit here!

"I'm with this sexy, brown skin, nice grain of hair black god. He's about 6 foot 4 inches with less than 10% body fat. This mother fucker is gorgeous, you hear me. He ain't nothing but the truth...

Now I'm sitting here cheesing like a kindergarten school picture. She covers the phone and asks me if it would be okay if someone joins us for lunch. I say of course.

"...yeah girl, we're at The Steak House in Georgetown. Okay, I'll order for you. See you in a few."

About 15 to 20 minutes go past. We're making small talk. I'm trying not to get myself in trouble. My boss already warned me. I'm a flirt. It's a curse. She's asking me what type of women I like. Making sure not to ruffle any feathers, I make sure to say I like them all sizes. I try to stick to common details like, nice teeth and feet, well manicured, attractive, and independent.

Before I can finish my description in comes this fine ass woman. I'm thinking to myself, please let this be who we are waiting for. Sure enough, she's making her way to our table. Mrs. Anderson stands to greet her. They hug and Mrs. Anderson introduces me to her younger sister. Now Stan said leave Mrs. Anderson alone, he ain't say shit about sexing her sister. She's about 5'6" but those Louboutin stilettos have her coming in at about 5"9. I know this woman has been a Jet beauty of the week! She's not wearing too much make up. It's not caked on like a clown. It's very light and tasteful. Me being the gentleman that I am, I pick my lip off the floor, close my mouth, and stand up to speak while pulling out her chair. She takes a seat while whispering to her sister that she was right on point about me. I just smile.

Ms. Anderson introduces us.

"Rhonda this is Felix... Felix this is my younger sister Rhonda"

We smile some more at each other. We all just started conversations. You know, making small talk.

"So Felix... who's the lucky lady in your life?"

"No one. ...I haven't found her yet. I'm not a firm believer in love. I don't think I'll ever find out what love feels like."

"You are just scared. But when the right one gets a hold of that ass, your through booking! You will be in love, sprung, and some more shit." Mrs. Anderson laughed

"I hope you're right. It's just that right now I have a problem trusting people. One day, I pray I'll be able to fully trust someone. Then I can really experience loving someone."

I purposely told them that shit because women love trying to change a mother fucker. They all think that their pussy is the one that can fix you. I lean in closer to Rhonda to hear her response. It was loud in the restaurant.

"So Rhonda...what do you do?"

"I'm taking classes....

My phone rang interrupting us. It's my office. I excuse myself before stepping away from the table.

"Hello."

Before I could even get the phone to my ear good, I can hear my boss chewing my ass out. I hung up without ever acknowledging that I could hear him. I played it smooth. I couldn't let them know my boss was pressing me like a baby mama for a Halloween costume.

"I'm so sorry ladies but I have to get back to the office."

"So soon?... I was just getting to know you" Rhonda purred.

"Hopefully, we can finish this discussion later. Mrs. Anderson it was a pleasure having lunch with you today. I will see you when you come by the office."

"You sure will. I want you to break his ass! I want every dime he has."

"Yes ma'm. Rhonda, here is my card... hope to hear from you soon. You ladies enjoy the rest of your lunch. This should take care of everything."

I gave Rhonda my business card and dropped two big face hundreds on the table like it was nothing. A soon as I hit the 5th floor, I can hear Stan is steady cursing me out. He's so loud; I can hear him as soon as I get off the elevator. He immediately begins to question me.

"Did you show her a good time?"

But the whole time he is still yelling and talking over me! I can't get a word in edgewise. Finally, he took a breath.

"Yes she loved me boss."

"Good... that's very damn good," Stan replied in a calmer voice.

"Don't worry... I got you covered." I assured him.

"We need this win right here to secure your promotion and for the company portfolio. You're going to be this firms youngest partner and I want people to know, you deserve it so get your ass back to work."

Walking back to my office my receptionist informed me that I have new messages. When I get back to my desk I sift through the messages. Ten of the fifteen messages were from my mother. Me being me, I'm thinking that something is wrong so I rush to call her back.

"Ma...what's wrong...what happened?" I say in a panicked tone

"Nothing... did you think about what I said earlier?"

"No Ma... but right now I can't get into this. My boss is digging in my you know what."

"Fuck him! You don't want to end up like him any damn way... grumpy and miserable."

"You right...but every day I see what being married gets you," I begin to laugh.

She got so mad she hung the phone up on me. So I go through the rest of my messages when I see Meka had hit me so I return her call.

"So how was breakfast," she asked in a sexy tone.

"It was great Hoover," I joked.

"Boy, stop playing."

"I'm not playing... you took the babies like an abortion clinic."

"Am I going to see you tonight?"

"I don't see why not, let's talk about this after work. I'm going to call you back."

"Okay baby."

I skip over the rest of the missed calls, I will get to them later. Time to get back to work getting everything lined up for Mrs. Anderson. I've got to make sure we are prepared for this case. I'm having a hard time focusing because her sister blew my mind. I'm mad as shit that I didn't get her number. Damn! I was slipping that round. That's okay though 'cause she was on a brother, so I know she's going to call me. I turned on some Maze and dug into the Anderson case.

Finally free 10 hours later. It's time to clock out and get started with my evening. I'm going to hit the gym, happy hour, and start over tomorrow. After work I meet up with some of my boys from the old hood. No matter how much money I get, I'm not going to change. You can take the man out of the hood but you can't take the hood out of the man. Every Monday I meet up with them, we shoot some ball then go to somebody's happy hour to have a few drinks with some nice women. We shooting ball reminiscing about growing up around the way. We used to bet on who can get the baddest chick. Of course it was always between Rick who is my older cousin and me. See my cousin Rick was the gambler/hustler/pretty boy out of the bunch. You know that women love a thug; especially a pretty boy. Don't sleep 'cause your boy was right on his heels. The only thing that held me back was that I would only dry hump. The kid was kinda scared of the pussy.

I don't believe I'm telling you this, but when my mother sat me down at 16 and gave me that shoe box with the kit, it was on! I was pressed to tell the team what she'd given me. The kit had motion lotion, edible condoms, regular condoms, handcuffs, sex dice, a pink vibrator, and a game called "take it off". My homies were jealous because they didn't get no shit like that. They could barely even talk to their moms about sex. Once I got that kit, I was on a mission. Your boy was turning out any chick that came his way.

We continued laughing and joking about all that while teasing my man Dink that didn't get no ass back then. That was then! Because now that shit done changed! His wife is bad as shit! Good Lord, that woman is fine as hell! We're still trying to figure out how he got her. That we'll never know but we're still happy for his funny looking ass. Further into the conversation, I bring up the young lady Rhonda I met earlier and how I want to draft her for my team.

"Every woman is a potential wife until you fuck her," I joke.

"You right about that," they all agreed.

"What did you say her name was?" Rick asked.

"Rhonda."

"What does she do for a living?"

"I didn't get to that part the last thing I heard her say was she was in school... why you fucked her?"

"Naw, I just know a Rhonda. Babygirl spent a lot of money with me. I think her folks or somebody in her family rich. Or, somebody passed away and left her some doe; I can't remember what it was. Either way she use to break bread with a nigga...but haven't seen her in awhile. Fuck it, I'm pretty sure that ain't her she wouldn't be traveling in the same circles as your boojie corporate ass. Wit' your Ph.D. hoes'... she ain't on that level."

"Damn bro, how you going to say the girl I like might be a crack head … that's fucked up Rick."

We all were cracking up.

"Man, let's just finish playing ball," Dink urged.

"Felix likes a once prom queen now a prom fiend," Rick joked.

Ya'll stupid… let's go shower up so we can go to the spot you dick heads."

We go hit the showers and head on down to happy hour. When I tell you that every top diva in the city will be in attendance that's what the hell I mean. As soon as we walk through the door the host greets us by name. She knows us because we come every week. She shows us to our table. Mind you it's the best seats in the house because you can see what comes through the door and its right across from the bar so all eyes be on the camp. If there was a VIP section, this would be it. But I think all eyes be on me because your boy be red carpet fresh, mints in the mouth, Chrome cologne on, and the shape up is so sharp you can file your nails with it. I have no problem buying any drinks or conversing with the ugliest chick in the building. Why? Because I'm confident that everything I want or touch turns to gold. That's why! This round I'm going to take a different approach. I'm gon' change the game with this move. Tonight I'm buying roses for every lady in the building and every ladies' first drink.

Well, let's just say it sounded like a good idea. Why did I do that? I bit off more than I could chew this time. Women are damn near jumping on my back trying to get at me. What they don't know is that I'm stunting. My name is going to be on the lips of every woman in this joint, even though I have hit a couple of them off. They love me! I have dibbled and dabbled in a couple of circles in my day. While I was sizing up this cute young lady who was in my face smiling and flirting, something told me to look towards the door. Who comes walking in but the school teacher Nikki and some of her co-workers. She was looking fine as shit! I mean drop dead sexy! I'm talking mouth open wide cute and every step she takes towards the bar is making my dick harder than ever. I never had a women do no shit like this to me. Her hair was in a pony tail. Her Chanel frames accented her beautiful round face and her business suit looked painted on. She finished the look with some Chanel pumps that had her legs looking like they went on forever. Not to mention, her ass was looking like the number 8 in that skirt. The first three buttons on her shirt were unbuttoned so you can see a little cleavage. Damn! I'm sitting here with my mouth watering like she's a steak as she walks pass me.

"Ain't that your folks? Damn…shorty looking good as hell. Tell her I want her buddy..." Said Rick.

So I flag her down and tell her and the buddies to come over to our table. I'm thinking as I watch them walking over, that I wish she would have gotten here earlier; she could have saved me some money.

"Hey boo… hey fellas."

"Hey."

"Wassup shorty. Please join us."

"Thank you."

"Nikki…what's your friends' name?" Rick asks.

"She's grown and can speak for herself so ask her."

"Miss Lady…how are you today?

20

"I'm fine."

"I can see that…what's your name?"

"Keisha… and you?"

"I'm Rick… would you like to dance?"

"Why not… I hope you don't have two left feet."

"I've been known to put a few feet in ER in my day."

We all laugh.

"Felix are you going to ask me to dance?" Nikki asks.

I lean over the table and whisper in her ear

"Fuck all that dancing and teasing me; meet me in the bathroom if you not scared."

"Aww shit Usher…so you want to make love in this club, huh?"

"You scared?'

"Boo, I ain't never scared! Let's see you put my nuts where your mouth is…"

"Shit… you know that I'm down like four flat tires."

She left first and went into the ladies room. I slipped the bathroom attendant a 100 dollar bill and tell her to watch the door. Tell people it's being worked on. I don't give a fuck what you tell them; just give me 15 to 20 minutes. This ain't the first time so she knows the drill. We're in this joint acting like were making a porno flick. I'm kissing on her neck. My tongue is in her ear. My hands are caressing her thighs. I grab her lifting her in the air sit her gently on the counter. She leans back and put her legs on my shoulders. I removed her thong and begin to tongue kissing her pussy. I take my fingers spread her lips a part and start doing my abc's on her clit. She is moaning louder and louder. Now her kitty kat is to the point that her glazed insides are running out onto the marble countertop. I whip out, put on a condom, and prepare to slide it in her.

"No, put it in my ass this time." She purrs.

I still went up in her to use her juices as a natural lubricant; I bent her over and slid it in. She tensed up a lil and clenched the sink for dear life.

"That's what you want baby, you like that shit huh?"

"Yes, yes, fuck me harder." She moaned.

So now my goal is to knock the lining out of that joint. I'm bringing her ecstasy to the point I see her reflection in the mirror and there's a tear in her eye. She's playing with herself, while I'm stroking like a professional guitar player. I'm breathing harder and harder. I'm about to reach my climax and she is reaching hers at the same time my man is about to explode. She screams out in pleasure and I wrap my hand over her mouth to muffle the sound. She bites the shit out of me. Now we're both out of breath huffing and puffing but we got to pull ourselves together so we can go back out there with the team to start mingling. I wipe the sweat off of me, flush the condom, and fix my clothes. She does the same routine. She wipes herself off, fixes her hair, and adjusts her clothing. I spray some more smell good, pop a mint in my mouth, and exit the bathroom first. Shortly after, she steps out. She can barely walk from that back door punishment she just took; we make our way back over the table.

Chapter 3

"What the hell is wrong with you Nikki?...What have you'll been doing?" Rick's hot ass says.

"Nothing" we both replied sounding guilty as hell.

"Ooooh, ya'll so nasty. Nik girl in the club though? It's like that? Must be nice...I ain't mad at cha! Must've been damn good," Keisha teased before giving Nikki a high five.

"Girl, you see me walking knock kneed. Girl, I need a nap, ya'll ready to go?

"You'll can go ahead and leave. I got Keisha. Nikki you know she's safe with me long as she don't try to rape me. It's hard trying to hold yourself together around a nigga like me. But if she does decide to do a lil' something with me I guarantee that in three minutes she will be screaming my name." Rick boasted.

"Sshittttt! If anything, in three minutes you will be sucking your thumb like a baby, you must not know playboy!"

Nikki and I cracked up laughing. They are crazy as hell.

"Well if ya'll are good, then we are out! I got a long day ahead of me with one of the biggest clients the company has ever had. Plus ya'll know I'm 'bout to make partner."

We all got ready to walk out of the door. I stopped at the bar to pay my tab when the bartender slipped me a note with a number. Once outside everyone said their goodbyes. Rick and Keisha disappeared down the street. I hailed a cab for Nikki, gave her a kiss and hug, and told her I would call her later. Then I hailed a cab for myself. During the ride home I just flashed back on my day and realized that I live a very blessed life.

The cab enters the circular driveway pulling up to my place. I paid my fare and walked into my building with the biggest smile on my face you've ever seen. Soon as I get to the elevator who do I see getting off the elevator with her dance bag and make up kit? Toya!

"So we meet again Miss Lady… it must be meant to be."

"What's meant to be?"

"You and I… enjoying a nice lunch or dinner and getting to know each other a little better?"

"I guess so just say when."

"How about Wednesday or Thursday?"

"Okay… that sounds fine."

She gave me her info, apologized for being short but she was running late. I kept it moving. I got on the elevator and went to my crib. I walked in and as soon as I lay across the couch my phone rang. I started to let that shit go to voicemail but I answered it. Good thing I did because it was Rhonda. She asked how was my night was going. I told her it was much better now that she was on the phone.

"I'm sorry my boss interrupted our lunch earlier. I didn't have enough time to get to know you."

"No need to apologize…you've got to make that money. So what did you do today?"

"After work me and a group of friends met up and played some hoops. We do this once a week. It's nothing like catching up with your friends. This suit and tie thing is my income but truth be told I was raised on the other side of the tracks."

"I feel you."

"Yeah, so every chance I get to see my partner, Rick we have good a time. You see we chose to different paths but I'm here for him to the end and vice versa."

"I know a Rick myself he was pretty cool."

"Funny that you say that, he said the same thing when I told him about you. He said he knew a Rhonda."

We laughed it off knowing he wouldn't know her. She's from the boojie side of the tracks. Besides there has to be a million Rhonda's and Rick's in D.C. So we talked a few minutes more and I told her that I'd had a long day and am getting ready to call it a night. We said our goodbyes and I promised to call her tomorrow.

I walked into my bathroom and turn my shower on. Aw, that's right. I looked in my suit jacket pocket for the napkin. I'd almost forgotten about the note my bartender slipped me. I began to read:

"I bet Ms. Thang didn't work you how I would have worked your ass in that bathroom. You need to trade up and fuck with a real stallion. When you're ready to be broken off correctly call me."

I put that shower on hold and immediately picked up the phone to find out who the hell this was.

"Hello?"

"I knew you would call."

"Which young lady were you?"

"Stay by your phone."

She hung up and just when I was about to call her back to see how we got disconnected, a picture message came thru. I opened the text. Well hello! It's a pretty pink pussy on my screen, and then the phone rings again.

"Hello."

"Do you like what you see?"

"Of course, how long would it take for me to see it in person?"

"About an hour or two."

"Let me see if I can wait up for that."

"Oh trust me, you're going to want to wait up for this!"

I gave her my address and hung up. The shower was calling me. So I jumped in and got fresh. When I got out I put on my Versace robe and laid across the couch. I dozed off. Three hours later the doorbell rings. I look through my peep hole to try to see what her mug is looking like. I can only see the silhouette of a phat young lady. Her body is ridiculous. For a minute, I got paranoid hoping it wasn't one of my women trying to trick me. Fuck it! I say a silent prayer that she isn't a wildebeest and get ready for whatever. I open the door, turn around and walk over to the sofa taking a seat without looking at her. Part of me wants to, but part of me doesn't. She enters and cuts the lights off. Good, this way if she's a gremlin, I can't be responsible for feeding her this dick after midnight. All I can see is a silhouette of her naked body. I open my mouth getting ready to talk and she shhh's me.

Then she pushes me back onto the sofa. She snatches open my robe. I'd just gotten out the shower before I laid down so I am still completely naked. She begins licking my nipples. She licks me all over. She went down my body skipping my dick and began to kiss my balls. Damn! Then she came up for a lil air put something in her mouth and began to give me some head. It took me a minute to realize that she was really putting a condom on me. That shit felt so good, I was lost. She climbed atop of me with her back turned to me. I couldn't see her face but she was definitely riding the shit out of me. She was leaning back so hard I thought it was going to snap my shit off. Then she starts bouncing on it until she felt that I was about to cum then she dismounted like a gymnast. Girl, what the fuck is your name?! She snatched the condom off and went to work. I thought what I had for breakfast was good, but the midnight bandit is trying to shatter her record. Then I let off the biggest nut in my life. I hurried up and flicked the lights on and to see who it was. Man, man ole' man, it's Toya! My midnight freak is my upstairs neighbor.

Standing here in shock, I'm trying to figure out what just happened. Wondering where all this came from? Honestly, I'm feeling used and turned out at the same time. Mostly, because she twirked the shit out of me. I'm talking that good type of sex that would make a nigga profess his love at the end. I gathered my composure then asked her:

"To what do I owe this extreme pleasure? What was all that for? Don't get me wrong, I enjoyed every minute of it! But, why did you do it?"

"A woman knows in the first 5 minutes of meeting a man if they would sex them or not. When I met you, I knew I wanted you."

Then just as mysteriously as she walked in, she just walked out.

"What does that mean?"

She paused for a second and looked back at me.

" Shhhh …keep it on the hush. Some things are better left unsaid."

I'm bout as confused as a midget in a NBA starting lineup. I feel lost and turned out. I can't even figure out a response. She left me speechless. I don't know how to feel about this shit here! I watched her disappear into the elevator and went back into my crib. Man, fuck it. I'm just gon' carry my black ass to bed. I'm drained. I guess with all that screwing I did today, a wet dream is out of the question tonight. As soon as I closed my eyes images of my sexcapade with Toya played repeatedly. I just kept replaying the shit over and over in my mind what Toya just did to me. I'm feeling some type of way but I don't know how to explain it. Let's just say I feel like a lady who gave it up on the first night now she's wondering if the dude plans on seeing her again. She got me fucked up! I can't sleep! I keep tossing and turning. I glanced at the clock, its 4:47am. I guess I must've finally drifted off because it's now 6 a.m. and my alarm clock is buzzing like crazy.

I'm super tired. I jumped up and hit the shower. For some reason I don't feel like talking and as usual my phone is ringing off the hook. I continued getting dress and ignored it. I put my shit on…you know, red carpet fresh as usual. I don't know who the hell this is blowing me up but my phone is constantly ringing. Now, not only is the phone ringing but so is the door bell. I let the phone continue to ring and go to answer the door. When I open the door there's a box with a single white rose and an edible thong. The note says, "If you're not scared…meet me on the rooftop."

Me being me, I ducks nothing! I ain't never scared! Right now, I don't care about being late for work, Mrs. Anderson and everybody else just gon' have to hold the fuck on for a minute. She manhandled me last night. I've got to redeem myself. I got work to do. I took off like a bullet and that wet-wet is the bull's eye I'm aiming for. The elevator was not coming fast enough so I ran up 5 flights of steps. I stopped to catch my breath before opening the door that leads to the rooftop.

When the door opens the first thing I see is this beautiful breakfast spread. Belgian waffles, turkey bacon, grits, you name it, it was there. This shit is laid out with some Moet Mimosa's and all. I was like damn. I walk over to sit my ass down and notice that there's another note. It's one of those folded cards type joints. The cover says, read me. So I read it. Its instructions:

1) Eat your food

2) Drink til you get a buzz

3) Take the 5 hour energy drink that's under the napkin

P.S. – I left some pictures for you to enjoy.

I open the envelope and take out the pictures. The pictures are of a faceless female advertising flexibility in positions I never knew could be obtained. She's on some cirque de sole' shit! The final pic was of someone naked with their legs open. On the back it said:

"Paint a picture in your brain until that soldier in your pants is saluting… then make your way over to the opposite side of the roof top where the sofas are. But…when you get here have your dick in hand ready to go."

Nigga what! I followed them directions to a T! I took a sec to call Stan and tell him I'd be in late, real late. When I get to the other side of the roof, dick in hand as requested, there she is! It's Toya. In a Burberry trench coat, butt ass naked with some red pumps on ready for action. No, not this time! Last night you got out on me but this time, I'm gon' make you speak Chinese. I grab her real tight, turn her to the side and start to gun her out till that thing is leaking. Then I put her on her back and bend her legs towards her head trying to make her ankles touch her ears. She takes them and wraps them around her neck like a scarf.

"Is this better for you…?"

Just seeing some shit like that had me ready to bust off. It's like a pussy pretzel. I thought that was just for the movies. I starting hitting that thang again but my Jedi mind trick ain't working, I'm about to let loose. She can see it in my face. I pull out real quick trying to calm myself down.

"…It's time to switch…my turn! Have a seat."

"Sure."

She stands over top of me and using the sofa arms to support her ankles, and she does a mother fucking split. No bullshit! She drops right down on me in a split position and starts bouncing.

"What's my name?"

"Toya"

"Whose dick is this?"

"Yours…baby it's yours"

"Can that bitch in the bathroom touch this pussy?"

"No…"

"Say you love this pussy"

"I love it!"

I can't take it no more. I fought a good fight but the pussy is cold bomb; I exploded. She got up with a smirk on her face, kisses me on the cheek and begins to close her trench coat. I can't believe the shit she had me saying! She had me calling her name like I was the broad. I leaned my head back closing my eyes for a few seconds to catch my breath and just like that, she's gone. What's up with the Whoodini disappearing tricks? Truth be told, I can see why that old man gave her all of his money. If she did any of this shit to him, she earned every dime! I'm trying to get myself together but my legs are like spaghetti noodles. Finally, I make my way back down to my condo. I'm thinking to myself, I have never had anybody fuck me like that. No one has ever done the things that she's doing. She's really turning me out. I'm not trying fall in love with her but if she keep doing shit like this I'm going to have a problem.

Keep in mind that my phone has been ringing constantly the whole time. When I answer, it's Stan once again chewing my ass out.

"Where the hell are you? You said you were going to be late not out!"

"I'm out doing my research …I have a meeting with a private detective who's willing to work on the Anderson case." I lied

"That sounds great…ok…well, hurry the hell up and bring me what I like when you come in to the office."

"What's that? Men?"

He was mad as shit and responded:

"Naw… your mother!"

He slammed the phone so hard it gave me a headache.

Chapter 4

I go wash up again, recoup, and get my gear on. For real, a brother needs a good 10 hours sleep. I need time to replenish. These chicks are wearing my ass out! Damn! I'm slippin'. I got to get it together with the quickness. I sat on the sofa for a few to regain some type of strength. Then I grabbed my briefcase and made my way down stairs. I snuck past Timmy who had his back turned helping another resident. I flagged a cab and was on my way to work. My phone starts ringing again. This time it's Rick so I answer.

"What's up bruh?"

"You wouldn't believe it if I told you?"

"Yeah…well let me tell you about Nikki's partner, Keisha."

"What happened?"

"Man, them lemon drops must've got her horny because shorty gave me some freeway."

"For real?"

"She whipped my dick out on the way to dropping her off home. She was going to work on it while I was driving. She was growling, like my joint was a steak. That shit felt so good, I almost crashed twice."

"Damn!"

"Man, she was a cannibal! She attacked that joint like she was starving and it was the last piece of meat on earth. I must say, her head game was on point. I was quite impressed," He laughed.

"Oh shit! Shorty showed up for work, huh?"

"She showed up and showed out!"

"Hold on my line is beeping...

I click over.

"Hello... wassup Nikki... I was just thinking about you."

"Is that right...well I called to tell you about your freak ass friend, Rick."

"Alright...hold on for a sec."

I click back over to Rick and tell him that I will hit him back in a few then I click back over to Nikki.

"...Now what was you saying boo?"

"Your boy is a freak...he stick his tongue anywhere."

"Why you say that?"

"Keisha told me that your boy suggested that they pull over. So they stop at this lil deserted park. He told her to get on the bench and he ate her out like he was at an all you can eat buffet. Homeboy was licking ass and everything."

"Are you serious?"

"Yep!"

Now I'm thinking to myself somebody lying or they both leaving out some shit to make themselves look good. I start laughing to myself.

"...what's so funny?"

"Nothing, I'm just thinking about something...baby I'm just pulling up going in the office; Stan is mad as hell at me. So, I'm gon' hit you back a little later."

"Okay baby...talk to you later. Don't forget to call me."

As soon as I flip the phone shut it rings again. This time it's Rhonda. I talk to her briefly until I made it to my office. I told her to meet me for lunch same place, same time. She said her class should be over by then and she'd be there. I rushed into my office. The first person I see when I walk through the door was Mrs. Anderson. She's in the lobby with Stan.

"I hear you out doing your thing to win this case for me."

"Yes... I sure am." I looked her dead in her eyes and lied like hell.

"Felix, my sister really likes you... so don't hurt her! She's been through a lot. She hasn't had it easy."

"Ok. I understand. As a matter of fact we are having lunch today after her class."

Stan is looking at me like, I know this mother fucker ain't doing what I think he's doing. Yes, Stan I am. I'm about to fuck the clients sister. And yes, I am two hours late and still plan on taking a lunch break. I walk to my office to do some research and some investigating. I start calling folks up and asking about Mr. Anderson's character trying to find out exactly who his mistress is. After a few hours of dead ends, I realize that I know the young girl that he is tricking with. My memory starts to kick in while staring at his picture. I've seen him in my building before. I can't remember the chicks name but he's paying for her spot. Timmy had mentioned something about him to me before. After my lunch date, I'm gonna call Timmy and see what information he got for me. Just as I was about to take a break my assistant buzzed in that I call on line 1 from my mother. I already know where the conversation is going to go. I still answer it.

"Hey ma how are you doing this lovely morning... well I'm late for a lunch meeting..."

"I'm great and blessed the Lord woke me up this morning. But, son I think I found the one for you. She's Ursula's niece. She's a nice clean girl not like them floozies you run with. She goes to church. She's is in the choir and everything."

"Ma...c'mon now... no more blind dates or church girls. I'm tired of looking like the devil on Easter Sunday after somebody in the congregation has been turned out. Ma, promise me, no more hook ups. Can we just have one conversation about anything other than my sex life, grandchildren, or relationships?

"Who the hell are you talking to? Boy, I'm your mother and I'll talk about what I want, whenever the hell I want. I want to know why I ain't got no damn grandkids? Everybody else got 2 or 3? What's the problem, you shooting blanks... you ain't on the lowdown are you? I know that boss of yours look kinda funny...he ain't get you to change teams did he?"

"Ma, c'mon now! You're going too far. I'm 1000% man."

"Ok Mr. 1000% gets me some damn grandkids then."

"Alright ma….I love you…I will call you later."

After that conversation I needed a drink or two! I went to go meet Rhonda for lunch. I want to really get to know her. When I arrived there she was already sitting and waiting on me. I glide on in there, take my seat and greet her.

"Good afternoon pretty lady…"

She breaks out speaking Spanish. I have no clue she said but I guess it meant good afternoon.

"…Well vole' vocu she' ava swa se swa…to you to."

She cracked up with laughter. I asked the waiter for my usual drink, Ty-Ku and Goose. I need to shake off the morning stress.

"So tell me about yourself?" I asked.

"Well, to make a long story short, my parents died in a train wreck. It's taken me a long time just to be able to say that. I've never fully recovered. I was their baby girl. I couldn't handle the thought of them not being here with me. They left me and my big sister enough money where as we would never want for anything. She married that sorry ass, no good for nothing nigga that used her for her money to start businesses and once he made some money he moved her out of the way for some young bitches. I'm only telling you this because she put him before me. She wasn't there for me like she should have been. 'Cause of that I had some bumps in the road trying to find my way. But enough about me, tell me about you?"

"My story is the same as every other hood dude. I was raised in the streets. I'm the only child but I had a lot of uncles and cousins that were in the streets.... so I had no choice but to have street smarts. The deaths of my god brother and one of my right hand men made me choose a different path. I was good in sports and an above average student so I took my money I made on the streets and went to college with it. After college, I went to Georgetown. I finished at the top of my class. After graduation I took the bar exam and here I am now. I've been working my way up and soon I'll be a partner. Other than that Ms. Lady, I'm just another black guy that escaped the ghetto."

"I know that's right! Well at least you made it."

"True dat'!"

I finished my drink and told her that I'd call her once I get off work. I reached inside my jacket pocket for my wallet.

"I got this one. I'm not the one that needs your money. I can pay sometimes. I'm not them other chicks looking for handouts." She laughs.

"I'm sorry baby... I wasn't trying to offend you. .. if I did please accept my apology. I was raised that a gentleman treats a lady."

"It's good to know that chivalry isn't dead... but this is on me. I want to treat you today."

"Will I see you later?"

"I hope so"

I kiss her softly on her neck and excuse myself to get back to work. While walking back I noticed a missed call alert. It was a text from Meka. I opened it up.

"Can I taste you?"

"Sure but it got to be quick."

I forgot who I was talking to. I forgot I was talking to the Hoover vacuum that will suck you dry. By the time I got to my office she was pulling up in her Escalade. I jumped in the front; we rode around the corner to the underground garage. I leaned my seat all the way back and she went to work. This was the first lady that I ever met that just enjoyed seeing me get off. She truly loves sucking dicks. I think I'll give her a new name. Yeah, I'll call her The Gobbler because she eats 'em all up and loves it. Between Toya this morning and Meka now, I'm exhausted. I don't think I have another nut in me. They done drained me dry. Man, I wanted to go to sleep in that damn truck but realized I had to go back to work. I'm glad Toya gave me that 5 hour energy drink but right now I feel like I'm down to 35 minutes. I had a boost for a little while. It was like Popeye eating his spinach. Either I better get another bottle or stop answering the phone. I walk back into the office to have my scheduled 3:00 meeting with Mrs. Anderson and go over some things for the case. I go and meet her in the conference room. I show her some things that I've prepared and we discuss how we are going to approach the situation. Losing is not an option.

"So how was lunch with lil sis?

My smile probably said it all. But you know I'm going to tell her what she wants to hear.

"It was good…I don't think I have ever ran into a more humble individual. She has so much character with a lot of insight on life. I learned a lot about her today. We've both had to face some serious trials in our time."

"So…she told you about everything?"

I was a little thrown by the question but I replied,

"She kept it on the up and up and told me everything."

"That's good… I never thought she'd open up about it and expose it all. I guess she has realized that you got to close the chapters to embark on a better future."

"I feel ya….so back to you… I need to know more about you and Mr. Anderson. What all has he done or said to you?"

"Well, first of all, he's been trying to keep me out of the loop about my money. He has secret investments and properties hidden from me. He's found a way to make decisions without me being there. He tries to sell me some bullshit about men don't respect women in the meetings so it's best that he goes alone. I'm not going to lie, I was young, dumb, and in love so I fell for that shit. Then I just started saying to myself, if I can't go then he's not going to get my money. He would get mad when I say stuff like that but that's how I felt."

"Well exactly how much money are we talking about? How many companies do ya'll own?"

"The money was part of an inheritance I received due to the death of my parents. At the age of 18, I was able to collect my part which was 5 million dollars. At the time, I was dating this waste of air and space guy that didn't even come to my parents' funeral. You know, he had the nerve to ask me to buy him a

Benz. When I told him no, he broke up with me. Then this loser I got as a husband now came along. He fed me a bunch of bullshit at the time when I was vulnerable. He worked me but I was too blind to see that. I married him after 6 months of dating. I'd never met his family or really knew anything about him. He had big dreams and ideas. He talked me into buying a movie theater and investing in stock. We took off from there. We brought some fast food restaurants, they did excellent. Next came a strip mall and with that we made a killing. By now we own half a monopoly board. But, the difference is this is real money. My 5 million has grown to about to 300 million. Somewhere along the line, I fell back and let him take over things. Now I really don't know what we have."

"Did you have a prenup?"

"No, but I got a Smith & Wesson. That's why I hired a private investigator. I found out this mother fucker was going on trips with women to all types of islands on private jets. He's buying jewelry, buying cars for them, and has the nerve to pay for these bitches a place to live. Believe me when I tell you, hell hath no fury like a woman scorned! So while he was sleep I went to the gas station, bought a gas can, and filled it up with 93 Octane. I drove back to the house that we spent 1.5 million dollars to build, walked into the bedroom, and started pouring. From the bed I made my way down to the front door. I took a lighter and lit it. When I tell u, God was watching over his sorry ass, whew! I think he smelled the gas and jumped out the window. The house went up in flames and that son of a bitch still survived. He deserved to die but I guess God wants him to suffer for what he did to me." She broke down into tears.

"Mrs. Anderson please don't cry. We will get him. But, do me a favor. Please don't tell that story again or you'll be in jail and he'll be out spending your money."

By now it seems like I might be getting soft and thinking about settling down. Hell naw! I snap out of it with the quickness. I don't do the love thing! Get yourself together Felix. Let me focus on the situation at hand. I give her some tissue before stepping out of the room to let her get herself together. While she is in there, I go to my office where my receptionist has once again left me a stack of missed calls and messages. I already know half of them are from my mother. Then the phone rings and sure enough it's my Mom.

Chapter 5

"Hello Mother… how are you doing on this nice bright day that the Lord woke us up to see and take part of?"

"The lord has blessed me as well …but son I know I promised you that I wasn't going to interfere with your personal life anymore… but we are having our annual couple's dinner on the 30th of next month. And, if you're coming this year please bring your own girl. Don't try to leave with somebody else's girl starting all that nonsense. And, by all means please, I say please leave Rick at home!"

"Yes, I'm coming and I got a lot of women to choose from….what happened last year wasn't my fault. The dude's girl wanted to leave with me. I mean I did come from you. But I promise this time I won't let anything like that go down. I got somebody that you will love. Ma, I've got to get back to work. I love you…I'll call you later."

"Okay baby."

I went through the rest of my missed calls. I see that Rhonda hit me up, so I called her back.

"Hey sexy …how are you doing"

"I was missing you so I hit you... but that's all I wanted. Smooches! Bye!"

It's nice to know that somebody thinks about me besides my mother. Right now, she's got the kid feeling special. That call sure put a smile on my face. I had a message from Toya. I'm trying to figure out how she got my work number, this bitch is vicious wit' it. I rushed to call her back. The way she's turning me out, you know I can't wait for what's next. She's got that make u want smack your mother kind of sex. The phone is ringing.

"Press the star key if this is Felix and wants his ass licked or press the pound sign if he thinks he can handle me giving him head while doing a handstand."

"Hello... did I dial the wrong number? I hope I didn't with these options. Do you have anymore?"

"I can fuck you a different way, everyday of the year..."

"Sshitt!...you do that and we getting married!...but for real though... how are you doing "

"I'm good just making sure that you're still breathing and that I didn't fuck you to death. I probably should warn you that I got a white liver. I can go all day every day."

"The whiter the better... so can I Miss Lady... besides I really think that you're running out of shit to do to me...but I will call you after I get off so that you can prove me wrong."

"We'll see then, won't we?"

Let me get my ass back to this meeting. I left her over thirty minutes ago. I'm pretty sure Mrs. Anderson is finished crying her soul out. I walked back into the conference room.

"Are you ok?"

"I just had a temporary mental breakdown….I'm okay now. It's just so hard when someone you love betrays you like he did. I have been holding back those tears for many days. I'm okay now…let's continue."

"I'm glad you're okay. I'm happy you got it off your chest so now we can move forward."

"I'm so glad you are defending me Felix. You have a great heart and very endearing personality. I will call you in a few days. I hate to end our meeting this way but I have to run. I have some things I must take care of today."

"No problem…I understand."

I walked her down stairs to her Maybach. After her driver pulled off, I rushed back up to my office to get my things ready for me to leave. While riding the elevator down stairs I decided to call Rhonda. For some reason I wanted to check on her. I wanted to let her know she ran across my brain. Just check and see how her day was, but when I called the phone went straight to voicemail; so I left a message.

"Hey sexy…I'm just sitting here picturing us walking through the park…you know chillaxin…so call me back when you get this message".

I hung up. Then my phone rang and I look to see who it is. It's none other than sexy ass Nikki. I'm really digging her. She's the type of female that is so chill. She's not needy. She doesn't call too much. She's a great single mother to her son. And most importantly, she just wants to build a great friendship with me you. If they had a report card for women, she would make the honor roll. Right now, I'd give her all B+'s with probably one or two A's. She's not the best cook but she cooks well enough for you to eat. She's not a label whore but she knows how to make anything she puts on look good. She's not that experienced as a freak but will try anything once for you. I guess what I'm saying is, she's right down the middle and that's what I like about her. She's not too extra with her shit. I push the button to answer her call.

"Hey boo…. how are you doing today? I know you have a tough job teaching those grown ass high school students these days."

"I know right… they are getting growner by the minute. I had to tell a young boy today to stop playing with me. His little ass is always trying to get fresh. Other than that boo, today was cool. I'm calling because I wanted to know if you wanted to go with us to the game with me tonight. I have 3 tickets and I would love for you to come with me and lil man."

"Sure…I would love to go. I'm just getting off. I'm on my way home. Meet me there in about an hour that will give me time to get home and change out of this suit."

"Okay baby…see you then."

I hung the phone up and made my way home. As soon as I hit the lobby I see Timmy. He informs me that he has a note for me from you know who. Actually I don't, I've got four women, which one is he talking about? I open it and it's from Toya. Attached is a lil fake credit card that reads, "Fuck me any way pass". The handwritten note says, use it when not scared. I thought to myself Toya stepping her game up. These peoples coming at me on another level! As bad as I wanted to use the pass right now, I'm gonna hold fast. I mess around the condo for a minute and finally get ready for the game. Truth be told, I really want to try my hand with Toya and say fuck that game; but that's the thinking with my hammer first side coming out. I shake it off and get myself together. I have a conversation with myself in the mirror. "Felix, just go enjoy yourself and do the family thing. The pussy ain't going anywhere. Did I just say "family thing"? I'm not married and damn sure ain't got no kids. Shit, I'm trippin! Let me get my shit together. My mind's playing tricks on me. My text message alert goes off. The message says:

"We're pulling up outside"

I grab my Gucci jacket and head for the elevator. I exit the building looking Dougie Fresh as usual and jump in the car.

"Wassup lil' man?" I said to her son extending my hand for him to give me some dap.

"Nothing." He replied giving me five.

We laughed and talked as we rode on out to the game. We arrived at the game, get in line, and guess who I spot from a distance, Meka. She doesn't see me but the line is moving fast so we are bound to see each other. I'm too smooth to panic so I tell Nikki that I have to go to the bathroom. I walk down to where Meka is standing with her girlfriends and I did some slick shit; I walked with my back turned and bumped into her on purpose. I acted like I didn't see her. After bumping into her, I turn around about to apologize. I acted genuinely surprised to see her.

"Hey baby…I didn't know you were coming to the game."

"Why you not here with her…who are you with? I thought I saw you earlier with a girl and a little boy." Her girlfriend nosey ass going to ask.

"I know you ain't up here with no bitch." Meka ghetto/ boojie ass screams loudly causing a scene.

"Man, kill that noise! I'm up here with my sister and nephew. You know his father ain't around…"

Keep in mind that I am an only child but she doesn't know that. To seal the deal with the lie, I call Nikki on her phone and tell her to look to your left until she sees me. She does and begins to wave.

"…You see the lady waving, that's my sister."

So Meka gullible ass waves back.

"She better had been your family or I was about to set shit off. I was going to fuck somebody life up."

"Man, you need to stop that insecure shit. I'll call you later."

I kissed her on her cheek and made my way back to Nikki. Nikki got questions as soon as I get back, but I was ready for her.

"Who's that… thinking she's about to be in a video?"

"That's my god sister and her groupie buddies. They're here trying come up off of one of these athletes."

I started laughing to myself thinking how slick I am. We go into the game and have a great time. The whole little family thing was pretty cool; especially since her son likes me. He's a good, smart, and talented kid. I whispered to him on the way to the truck.

"If Mommy have any dudes come over there make sure you call and tell me."

"I got you."

Chapter 6

So as we were leaving, Nikki mentions that she's got something to show me.

"Ok… show me!"

She stops in front of me and lifts her shirt up in the back and said I got that tattoo you wanted me to get. I was shock because she got my favorite character, "Felix the Cat". It's the same tattoo Meka has in the same exact place.

"You fuck with me huh?"

"I have been trying to tell you that."

"Who did it?"

"Your folks… Vino Black did it."

"Cool! He did a great job on that joint. It's looks real good."

So we get in the car, I'm driving, and lil man goes straight to sleep. Next thing I know my zipper comes down. Out comes my Trombone and she starts blowing all the right notes. She got so into it to the point her slurping was getting too loud. I had to turn up the music up so lil man wouldn't wake up. When I tell you she never went this hard, she has NEVER went this hard. She went to the point where she had tears in her eyes. She had that "I love you" head. It's like she was on the internet all day researching how to give great head because she had it down packed. When I let all my fluids go, I almost crashed into a tour bus. But, you know I maintained. She licked me clean like she was possessed. She's hungry for this meat. She's still trying to keep going but I couldn't take it anymore.

Needless to say, instead of me going home I went over to Nikki's house to finish what we started. This is like my 100th time over here but tonight seems to be different. We pull up in to the drive way. I picked up lil man and carried him in the house. I laid him in his bed after taking off his shoes and coat. For a minute, I just stood there looking at him like he is my son; still picturing this family thing. I walked down the hall to Nikki's room. When I get in there she is butt naked pouring candle wax on herself. There's a fresh bowl of cold fruit on the bed beside her. The window is open a lil so it's a slight breeze coming through. Between the breeze and the way I'm kissing on her back, its sending chills through her body. Her knees were even shaking. I slowly spread her legs apart and slid into the warm wetness. I begin stroking to a melody in my head. I don't know what song it is, but with every stroke the melody is getting clearer to me. It's Guys', "Let's Chill." In my mind I'm singing:

"Let's chill…let's settle down, that's what I want to do"

See that's how you last a lil longer. You take your mind off of sex and think about other things. But, if you run across a young lady with that wet shit, then that strategy goes out of the window. In that case, you got to pound her until her body is numb and she is shaking like she's have a seizure. Then after that punishment she'll fall into a deep sleep with a smile on her face.

After our long night of wrestling, because that's what she told her son we were doing, I left to go home. By the time I got home I realized it was best for me to work from home today. I'm tired, worn out, and I think I'm coming down with a cold. I'm moving sluggishly because I'm really beat. As I'm getting on the elevator I see Toya running to catch it. I started to let the door shut but I didn't. As soon as she enters I can tell she's about to say some freaky shit. As soon as the door closed she said:

"I see you were scared to use that pass."

"Never that… I'm just tired… believe me, I runs from no one."

"OK…let's see…

Just then she hit the emergency stop button on the elevator.

"…you can't run now. So what you going to do… you know I don't have any panties on…"

I used what little bit of energy I had left in the tank to lift her up onto the railing. I fucked her like we were reenacting Monsters Ball.

"…Make me feel good." She hollered over and over.

And indeed I did. That was until I bust off and nearly dropped her ass because I was so weak. We got ourselves together and I was thinking to myself how much I really like this girl. She does the shit that average women are afraid of. You will find yourself cheating on your wife because of the things she down for. I got off the elevator and barely made it to my crib. I walked through the door and collapsed onto the couch. My sleep was being constantly interrupted by phone calls. I kept ignoring them because my body was tired. I just don't feel good. Not to mention, my right leg keeps shaking from the sex I just had. That's how I know I had some great good good. My phone continues to ring so eventually I answer. My sickness is coming down on me so my voice is so raspy.

"Hello… who is this?"

"It's Rhonda …you sound terrible…what's wrong?"

"I'm having body aches and sick as hell."

"I can't leave you there sick with no one to care for you.

"My class is over so I'm on my way, baby. Text me your address and I'll be there in a few."

I text her my address and go back to sleep. I feel like shit! Body hurting! Head spinning! I got the cotton mouth. My mouth is dry as shit. The door bell rings forcing me to get up. I feel like I have been in a fight with 10 Mike Tysons. Somehow I manage to make it to the door. Rhonda comes strutting through the door looking sexy as shit. She has a strut like she has her own theme music playing in her head.

"Aww baby you look terrible. I don't like to see you like this."

"I'm good boo… I think."

I break into a coughing spell and start barking like a dog,

"Have you taken anything yet…if not I brought you some Nyquil, Robutussin, and Theraflu? Whatever you want I got it for you. I'm going to take care of you one way or another.

C'mon let's get you into bed…then I'm going to make you some homemade chicken noodle soup."

I give a half smile because it really hurts to give a whole one with these body pains. I put my arm around her shoulder and we made our way to my bedroom. A little later she arrived to serve me in bed. When I tell you she has made me the best soup ever; believe me. That soup was off the hook. Besides my mother, no female I've dealt with ever took the time out to do the little things like making me some damn homemade soup. That's when I start to see that she has the old fashion morals and principals. She's demonstrating a lot of characteristics that my mother and grandmother have that are hard to find these days. Like she believes in letting a man be a man; that a man is the head and the women is the tail. I told her that she reminded me of the women from back in the day and how they carried themselves.

"I was taught that its certain things a lady should just no how to do. No matter if you have more or, make more than your man, you still let him believe he's the bread winner. You never crush a man's pride…nowadays woman believe so differently. They are screaming miss independent and they are the ones that are most miserable because they get so caught up within themselves that their ego out grows the man that they are with. That's why there are so many lonely women with only material things to keep them warm at night."

"Ok …I feel you on that."

I let out a loud yawn. I took some Nyquil and it was over. The medicine put me out. The smell of Pine Sol woke me up. When my eyes finally focused I glanced around and noticed my condo was spic and span. I'm talking see your reflection in the hardwood floors clean! I see Rhonda with her lil yellow gloves and pink bandana looking like a Stepford Wife. She's a totally different person from what I thought. But, what's fucking with me is the fact that I texted Meka, Nikki, and Toya telling them I was sick. Not one of them offered to bring me the littlest thing. No tissue, soup, or juices; no nothing! This is forcing me to see that those bitches ain't shit. They're just looking for a good fuck. I can't hold a grudge against them. They might have some personal problems or going through something. Or, they might have been busy. Either way it's cool!

"Baby since you're up… sit in this chair for me…so I can change your sheets… where do you keep the spare sheets and stuff? Never mind I found them."

She changes the bed linen before offering to help me back into bed. I stay in the chair. Then two minutes later she walks past me with my clothes hamper going to the laundry room to wash my clothes. When I tell you every minute she is doing something to make me see what kind of woman I want in my life, she is definitely the front runner. The day is coming to a close.

"I want you to stay with me tonight."

"I don't know if that's a good idea. I don't really know you like that. We just started dating and I think it might be too early for that."

"What do you think I'm going to do to you?"

"I don't think you would hurt me or anything like that. I just don't want you to get the wrong impression of me."

"If you don't want to stay, it's cool. I guess I can manage with my body hurting and me feeling like I'm going to cough up a lung. Just make sure you call and check on me, I should be alright."

"I will stay... but I'm not fucking you."

"Girl... I wasn't thinking about sexing you," I lied.

In the back of my mind I really was. I walked off to the shower and my joints were stiff as ever. I left my towel on the bed by accident so I had to double back. While washing up I noticed my bathroom door opens and shuts quickly. I laughed to myself. I finally get out the shower and walk to my bed butt ass naked. I didn't know she was lying across my bed. So, I grabbed my towel and began to dry myself off. She doesn't know that I've caught her eyes on me. Every time I turned to look at her, she turns her head towards the TV. Mind you, I'm packing something nice. She can't help but stare at this third leg I got.

Chapter 7

I grab my cologne, my lotion and everything else I put on at night. I take my time putting it on so that it can soak into my pores and be nice and seasoned. I put on my robe even though most of the time I sleep naked. I laid across my bed opposite of her. As soon as I hit the bed she rubs her foot across my legs. Her feet are soft and pretty. She doesn't have any corns. My mind is telling me to lick them joints but I just chill. Then she catches herself. She was about to slip up and let the good girl role go out the window. I wasn't mad that she stopped because I'm tired as hell and starting to dose off from the medicine. It's kicking in real subtly. I feel her rolling out of the bed and walk into the bathroom and turned on the shower. I assumed she got in because I've been snoring like a bear. I sleep light so when she walked past me I opened one eye to peek. She didn't know that I'm watching her so she dropped the towel and stood there ass naked putting lotion on her body. Damn! She is phat as all out doors! She looks like she belongs in a video. I just know that she's about to put on a t-shirt or something but she comes and lies beside me with no clothes on. Her back is to me. Thinking that I'm asleep, she puts my arm around her. Me being the freak that I am, I turn on my side so my robe can move and my soldier can nestle against her soft ass. Hopefully that will turn her on to the point she would want to do something. Needless to say, that trick didn't work! We just laid there sleeping till the alarm clock went off.

We both wake up. You know the first thing a man has to do when he gets up…go to the bathroom. When I come out to lie back down, I notice that she isn't in the bed, but I smell food. I immediately make my way to the kitchen. She's in there getting it in. Making everything from scratch! She must've gone to the store because some of this shit I KNOW I didn't have in the fridge.

"Baby why don't you go lay back down…you're food will be ready in a minute."

"Alright…"

I walk behind her and kiss her softly on her neck.

"…thank you."

A few minutes later she arrives with a tray of home cooked food and my newspaper. I think I've found my future wife, if she keep this shit up. She's doing everything right! On top of that, this is the first time in my life that I've ever laid in a bed with someone and didn't sex them. I call Stan:

"Hey Stan… I will be working from home the rest of this week. I'm not feeling to good. Can you have everything transferred to my home phone? Have the receptionist send my case files by courier as well."

"You better be working hard for Mrs. Anderson. You know what's at stake. I hope you get better son…if you got that swine flu that's going around keep your ass home!" he laughs.

"That's cold! Naw…I'm good. I'll be in touch"

I went back to relaxing and reading my newspaper. Rhonda cleaned the kitchen and announced that she was leaving.

"I'm going to go home and change. I have to get ready for my class."

"Why don't you stay with me today? You can miss a class...or two!"

"I can't miss my class. I need my education..."

The way she said it you can tell she felt some kinda way so I left it alone.

"...Do you want me to call you to check on you?"

"No... I want you to come back over later on to check on me personally."

She paused while walking towards the door and looked back over her shoulder at me.

"Okay...I really enjoyed spending time with you."

"Me too Miss Lady."

Just like that she was gone. The door closed. I sat on the couch where I was about to finish reading and my door bell rang. I ran to the door thinking Rhonda might have left something. Or, she changed her mind and took me up on my offer to spend the day with me. I snatch open the door and boy was I wrong. It's Toya standing here naked with some heels. My mouth drops to the floor.

"You go hard if you came down stairs like that! Did anybody see you?"

"I don't know and damn sure don't care if they did. Now, are you going to keep me out here in the hallway or can I come inside and play. I saw your lil girlfriend leaving. Now it's my turn to take care of you, since you are sooo sick."

I hurry up and pull her inside. Mind you, I still have on my robe so it's easy access. She spins me around pinning my back to the door. Then she just drops down into a split and begins to give me head. I have had a lot of women to go down on me but never had anyone to drop into a split. This is definitely a first. Then she did a stripper move and ended up in a handstand. Her legs rested on my shoulders and her Niagara Falls was right in my face. I had no choice but to tongue kiss her second set of lips until she is ready for a 4th of July explosion. Before I could get her there, she breaks out another move. The way she twisted her body and slid down mines, was unbelievable. It was like I was the pole. She landed in a position where she is bent over, ass in the air, lips spread waiting for me to sink the battleship.

As I began massaging her insides, she's begging me to go harder and harder. Her moans grow louder and louder. Some air gets in her vagina mixed with the pounding and wetness and it starts to make that farting sound. In a man's mind that does something to us; that's when we know we're putting in some good work. Now I'm pounding like a jackhammer and she loves it. They say when you are sick the medicines prolong you reaching your point. I'm going to test that theory out. I go into overdrive. By this time I have picked her up and pinned her up against the wall face first. Her breast just going up and down on the wall! I'm up under her dipping and stroking. I'm talking shit, pulling her hair. I choke her a little, put my finger in her mouth and then in her ass. Now she's really screaming. She's begging me to stop because she doesn't want to cum, but I can't. I'm still stroking; feeling like Biggie getting deeper and deeper. She was about to cum so I back up like she told me to. She came and it squirted out. What fucked me up was the fact that she just urinated on my $10,000 dollar cashmere rug. That's how she cum's? This shit really, really freaked me out. Never in my sexual life have I experienced this type of orgasm from a woman before. She realized that I still haven't let one go so she told me to go sit on the couch. I'm trying to get back in the moment but I'm mad as hell about my rug.

She walks over to me. She notices some candy on my coffee table. She grabs a Altoids, lays me back onto the couch, and put her face in my lap. See when she put that Altoids in her mouth it changed the way her head felt. It seemed like my pores were open; like when you put vapor rub on your chest. I told her she can't have no male friends, no boyfriends, as a matter of fact she can't even strip no more. That thing is too crucial! I want that all to myself! I think when I exploded it shook the building. I can tell that she's feeling me more and more now. Because, this time she didn't get right up and leave; she stayed for second.

"I was thinking about giving up the pole anyway… so I guess I got to do it a lot sooner, huh?"

"Damn skippy!"

She picks up her pumps and leaves. When I tell you I **have never** met a female like this, I mean just that. She's vicious to the point that I had to call my man, Rick. I'm still aware that even though he's my man he always tries to one up me on everything. The phone is ringing.

"Hello… what's good bruh? What's poppin' on your end?"
"Man… I just had this vicious one. A real live wire that did it all splits, handstands, back bends, giving me head with Altoids in her mouth… and she took it in every whole."

"You too playboy?... I had a mean one last night myself! She was giving me head while I was playing Madden… then she did a back flip off the bed, landed on my lap and she put a TV remote in her ass."

I'm looking at the phone like "this mother fucker here". I shake my head as he continues with his lie. My line beeps and it's Nikki. I tell Rick that I'm going to call him back. Then I click back over to Nikki.

"Hey boo... I'm down stairs with Timmy."

"C'mon up baby."

I wait two minutes to give her enough time to get on and off the elevator before opening the door. Here she comes down the hallway with both hands full with grocery bags. She has that certain walk with her that just leaves you stuck. She comes through the door smelling so damn good. I kiss her on the cheek.

"Why aren't you at work today?"

"School was out plus I felt terrible about not being here for you while I know you are sick."

"It's cool...I understand that sometimes we all have other things on our plate."

We're in the kitchen. She's sorting the groceries out.

"Baby I have a question....since we've been dating so long...some years now...where do you see this going? I just want to know..."

"Well boo... you know I got feelings for you and your son, but honestly I don't know."

Total silence filled the room. For a minute, I thought I went deaf. It was so quiet you could hear a rat pissing on cotton. You can tell she was feeling some type of way now. She wouldn't even look my way. I left her in the kitchen trying to give her a few to cool off. I walked to the bathroom, and hopped in the shower. While I was in the shower she left without saying a word. All I heard was the door slamming. I jumped out of the shower tried to catch her. I called her phone and she sent me straight to the voicemail. On the 4th call she finally answered the phone.

"What the hell do you want Felix? You don't appreciate me… so I'm going to find someone who does! I'm going to do me."

Click! The phone went dead. I sat on the bed and tried to figure out what went wrong. I mean, I'm young and living life. I'm not ready for that love shit. She's talking 'bout "she going to do her", well get the hell on! I got a list of women I'm not gonna trip off losing one. Now she done really sparked the flame. She out here playing like I'm not the man! Shit its 30 women to 1 man, out here! One girl fuck up, I got 29 more tries. As soon as I made my mind up to kick her ass to the curb, I receive a text from Nikki.

"Just know that I loved you! You shitted on me and my feelings! Don't worry about replying just have fun with being a ladies' man."

Then my phone rings and I think its Nikki . Wrong! It's Meka!

"Did you forget that you're supposed to accompany me to my co-workers engagement party at the GayLord Hotel tonight at 7:30?"

"No… I didn't forget. I'm just a little sick. But, I'm good now boo. I will meet you there."

"Baby please be there no later than 7:15. The attire will be on point sharp as ever… and dress to kill. So I guess I will see you there… bye sexy."

I try to shake the Nikki shit off and go back into relax mode. I'm in a daze thinking 'bout Nikki. Fuck it! There's no use in crying over spilled milk, got to be the playa that I am. I laid down for a while until it was time to get red carpet fresh and go to this affair. I plan to shut it down like I do on a regular basis. When I arrive it's about 7:05. I see Meka talking to her co-workers in the lobby area and as soon as she notices me her whole glow changes. She gets a big Kool Aid smile. I overhear one of her other co-workers telling her how fine I am. That was my cue to walk up to where they're standing. Me being me, I start to greet everyone.

"Ladies, how are you doing… I'm Felix."

Then I extended my hand out to shake hands with everyone. One particular friend grabs my hand and was not trying to let it go.

"Oh… you smell so good." The young lady purred

"I smell gas," Meka snapped as she snatched my hand back.

They didn't know what that meant; but I did. She told me a long time ago, *"if we're together and things are not going right let me know. Because, if you cheat and I catch you with the bitch I'm throwing gas on her ass! Poof she's going up in smoke. We'll see how much you like the fried side ho then."* Since then, when we are around each other and females begin to flirt, she always makes that remark. We walk in the event and have a seat where we see our names reserved on the plates. We're sitting with a bunch of married couples. They're asking us if we're married or engaged.

"No… not yet."

I'm looking at her like, how about no…not ever! When was she going to tell me that we were getting married? I start to look around the tables at all of the men. They all are looking depressed and sad. They look as if they have a chain and ball around there ankle. I'm thinking to myself to get through this night, it's a must that I pay the bartender a visit. I excuse myself from the table then make my way over to the bar.

"Hey bartender...it's an emergency... I need to double shots of patron. Follow that with whatever you got for me."

"Drink this... you will love it."

"What   is   it?"
"It's called "Come fuck me"."

"Well ok! That sounds good to me."

I make my way back over to the chain gang table, have a seat, and listen to the old ladies give Meka tips and pointers on marriage; for what, I don't know! I guess she's jumping the broom with somebody...won't be me. I drifted off into thought about what my mother calls and say to me every single day. Is it going to be Nikki or Rhonda? Shit if Toya stops stripping she might be the one. I snap out of that quickly. My minds playing tricks on me again! Shake it off! Whatever that bartender gave me has got me feeling real horny and the dance floor is calling my name. I grab Meka's hand and take her to dance with me. The DJ is rocking one of my favorite songs by Frankie Beverly and Maze, "Before I let go." What was once a boring affair now has a little life to it. It's rocking up in here or I'm just twisted. So now, I'm freaking and putting my tongue in her ear; making her wet as ever.

"Boy stop that. You're doing something to me."

"Are you scared?"

"Scared of what?"

"Scared of getting hot and going out by the water and pulling a "Jayson Lyric" move."

"Out front?" she whispered.

"Yeah! I've already peeped out the spot under a tree…plus it's dark. You down?"

"Didn't I get the tattoo?"

"You do have Daddy's name tatted on you. That means that kat is mines anyway… so come on."

We slide out the side door while everybody is doing their one, two step. I don't think anybody noticed us. We crept down the hill to this little secluded spot. I laid my jacket on the grass. Then I laid her down. I slide her heels off and began to lick every sexy ass pedicured toe. I started to kiss up and down her calf muscle. Then I unzipped her dress and let it fall down. She's not wearing a bra or panties because of the way the dress was made. I softly began to kiss on both nipples until they are harder then nails. My tongue traveled down to her stomach and I begin to kiss around her belly button. I lick every part of her, all the way down her happy trail. I notice her river is overflowing. Her juices are running down her leg. Damn boo! Did I do that to you? Next thing you know, we are really rolling around in the grass. Her kat it's so juicy it's making that squishy sound. You hear the waves in the water hitting the wall. She's getting louder as that thing is about to cum. Suddenly, her flood gates open. That thing almost drowned me. Just as I'm about to reach my point, I hear some laughing. I look over my shoulder and it's some Chinese tourist taking pictures of us getting it in. She's embarrassed as hell, trying to put her clothes back on. But me being me, I'm trying to finish what I started.

Chapter 8

"Boy stop!"

"Hell naw! You got yours, I need mines! Fuck them... they don't speak English anyway. It's not like we're going to see them again."

"Felix, boy…. just get your ass up! I will finish you off later on. You got me out here being the poster child for porn."

"Girl I swear it didn't happen like this in the movie. Okay baby, I'm going to get up but you better finish me off. I don't want to be walking around with two big watermelons in my pants. I need to get this off.

"Hurry up…it's about to rain."

Rain came pouring from the skies. We rush to get our shit on and break for her car. The tourists are all clapping, like we just gave them a hell of a performance. She is so embarrassed that she's running to her vehicle with her face covered and cursing me out; I can't stop laughing. We make it to the car and she starts drying off. I'm sitting here watching her wipe her legs. It's like everything is in slow motion. The water is just dripping down her neck onto her breast. In my book she's damn near a stripper, the

4Play

way she is taking her clothes off. She looks so good I'm mesmerized. I want to say something but the words won't come out. I feel like a young fella that never had sex before and I've just seen my first set of breast and coochie.

"Fool why you looking at me like u ready to bite and eat me?"

"Because I am! So I need you to pull over to the nearest parking space."

As we are parking, T pain's "Back Seat Action" came on. One thing I know is music always give you signs and directions to what you and your partner are supposed to do. So I make sure when a song is playing I do as they say. It's still raining.

"C'mon let's get out"

"Baby, you just got over being sick"

"I'm a grown man…don't worry about that. C'mon"

The rain lightens up a little bit and she gets out. I grab her gently, lifting her onto the hood of the car. We start kissing and biting. Then I lean her back to where her upper body is on the windshield and I begin to nibble on her kitty kat. The thunder is rumbling. I can tell her orgasm is coming closer and closer to the point she is about to explode. I stop just before she came. I climbed onto the hood of the car and pushed her up onto the roof part. I slide between her thighs. Now the rain starts to come down harder. The thunder is getting louder. I'm digging deep in her. I'm pounding to the point that she's breathing for me. She can't get her words together; it's like she is speaking in tongues. A flash of lightning struck nearby. It scared the shit out of me. The look on her face let me know, I better not stop. The lightning struck even closer to the truck and she came. It felt like an atomic bomb went

67

off. She was shaking like she was having a seizure. When we finished, she was stuck laying there. Her eyes are fixed on the sky. Rain drops landing on her face.

Finally, she got her self together and we drove off back to my house. The entire ride she was silent. I glance at her every 15 minutes or so. I caught her a few times shaking like she's catching the Holy Ghost.

When we arrive at my building and I see Toya walking past with a couple of bags going inside. She winks her eye at me and I wink back; not thinking Meka peeped it.

"Don't get that bitch slapped! Disrespecting me like that! As a matter of fact, I'm going to say something to her myself," The car door flew open so quickly, I had to come up with something fast.

"Cut that shit out! You too grown to be acting like that. She wants what you have! Don't feed into that."

"I guess you're right but I was sure going to ask her if she wanted to fuck you or something."

"Naw… she's just friendly," I laughed.

"How friendly has she been to you since defending her?"

"It's not like that at all…c'mon now baby… just give me a hug and kiss so I go in the house."

When she finally leaves I enter the lobby. Almost like she's waiting for me, she's still in the lobby. She and Timmy are talking.

"What …are you moving out?"

"I decided to take a friends advice and leave the heels and pole alone."

"You don't have to leave the heels behind." I said as I walked to the elevator.

I wink at her before the doors closed. As soon as I get up on my floor the phone rings. It's Rhonda asking if I wanted any company.

"Why not… I'm just about to walk through my door now. Come on over. The door will be unlocked so come on in; I might be in the shower."

I go inside and jump in the shower. I'm going hard with that Chrome body wash. I've got to get that pussy smell and that outdoor rain scent off me. The bathroom radio is playing Lenny Williams, "I love you." I'm singing along with it too.

"Girl you know I… I… I… love you…no matter what you do…"

Suddenly, I feel a cold breeze come through. I can tell my bathroom door has opened up. I can see a shadow through my bathroom curtain. The curtain slides back and someone steps in. I turn around and it's Toya!

"How did you get here?"

"Nobody supposed to be here…" she burst out singing the Deborah Cox song.

"Shawty, you wild."

"You left your door unlocked for me right?"

I'm looking at her like a paycheck. Damn, she's cut up like dope. She's sheer perfection from head to toe. She's standing here

A.J. Williams

with the perfect body. I really want her to stay but I can't risk the chance of Rhonda coming in. I have to think fast. I hear the front door open and close.

"Toya….my mom's just walked in. … I need you to walk out the bathroom into my bedroom while I walk into the hall way from the other entrance and distract her. I'm gon' to take her towards the kitchen." I whisper.

The shit was working well until the bathroom door opens. Lucky for me, it's so hot and steamy that she couldn't see anything in front of her. I'm nervous as shit! I'm not trying to show Toya that I can't handle pressure; knowing that I'm built for situations like this. Just as she's about to get out the shower, she starts licking my Chico stick. I want her to stop, but at the same time, I'm like naw don't stop. My hand is on the back of her head. She's using every deep throat trick she knows. I mean, I'm clearly in the back of her throat. I get the strength to pull her up by the ponytail and tell her she has to go. I reassure her that I'm not putting her out; she just can't stay in here right now. This is some hard shit, I really want her to stay but a playa has got to play. I open the door to my room to peep things out and see the coast is clear so she runs into my room. I open the other door and see Rhonda headed for my room.

I get her attention and wave her into the bathroom. She turns around, runs towards me, and jumps into my arms. While she was hugging me in the bathroom, Toya crept quietly out the front door.

"Who were you talking to in the bathroom? I could have sworn I heard a female voice?"

"Naw, that was the radio baby! That was Tina Marie and Rick James, "Fire and Desire playing."

70

"I see your fire is turned on the way your sidekick is alert. Other than that... are you feeling better?"

"I'm not feeling better at all. My body is hurting like I have gone through 3 weeks of basic training."

"Oh really?"

"All I need is some good loving, some affection, a little bit of that bomb homemade soup, and a warm bed. I will be good after that."

"Well, I can help you with the bed and soup. The other things you need... you might have to phone a friend."

"Oh really?"

"Before I forget... my sister asked how her case is looking?"

"Tell her we got this one in the bag. I'm going to lay down my body hurts."

I walk to my room in disbelief. I let a sure thing leave for a maybe. Walking to my room I start thinking about how I haven't heard from Nikki. She must really be mad. I send her a text.

"Baby, I miss you. Ur on my mind. Hit me back"

Two minutes go by and still no response. I pick the phone up about to call her and Rhonda walks in the room with the soup. After my little adventure in the rain, I still have to eat it to knock this cold out of me. I'm lying in my bed watching my favorite movie, "Harlem Nights". It's on the best part, when my man gets turned out by Sunshine. Every man I know wishes they'd run into a Sunshine. Out of all these years on God's green earth, I would never think I'd meet someone whose sex drive is higher than mines. That was until I met Toya. She could make a person change their religion, smack there mama, and go to hell and back for the shit she do.

Rhonda is lying at the foot of the bed; curled up.

"Why don't you come up here and lay beside me…"

She's acting all scared and nervous.

"… stop acting so anti…you act like I'm going to bite you or hurt you or something."

"I'm not these typical women your used to. I've only been with 3 men in my life. I haven't had any sexual contact with anyone in 3 yrs. The last person abused me and my soul both physically and emotionally. He knew that he had me to the point where I would do anything and I mean anything for him."

Then she begins to break down crying. Now what was supposed to be sexy turned into me consoling her; lying to her about being different from the rest of them clowns she dealt with before. I fall asleep on her and about 30 minutes into my sleep, I can feel someone starring at me. I open one eye and she is laying on my chest looking right at me.

"Don't hurt me," she whispers.

She begins kissing on my chest and then my six pack. Now she's really using her tongue! I can tell that she's ready to stop fighting this attraction. Then she goes down to my Mt. Rushmore and kissed my president. Her mouth action has my toes curling. I can snatch the sheets off the bed with my ass, that's how tight I'm squeezing. What happened to the saint? She went further down and ran her tongue across my ass with this fast motion. Then she moved back up to my shaft going slow, and then fast like a bobble head. It's about to be like Independence Day in my lap. She abruptly stops and climbs on top of me; straddling her legs over mine. She inserts my USB into her hard drive.

I'm so deep in her I'm leaving prints on her tummy. She's clawing and moaning. Her hips are rotating like she is playing with a hula hoop. It feels like her body is doing some tornado type shit. I'm stuck in a trance because she really had me fooled. While she is riding me, I scoot towards the end of the bed until I felt I was on the edge. On queue when I stood up, she wrapped her legs around me. I was feeling like Ving Rhames on *Baby Boy*. I've always wanted to try that move so I'm really in the zone. We start hopping around the room before I pin her ass up against the wall. We went at it until we both exploded falling out on the floor. Then we passed out in each other's arms, sweating bullets and breathing like bears.

I wake up because I can feel her shaking and scratching her body. I start thinking that maybe she's cold. I get off the floor and try to gather myself. I scoop her into my arms, place her on the bed and pull the covers over her. But she's still shaking like she's experiencing a bad dream or something. I lay down beside her, wrapped my arms around her and then began to rock her. I rubbed her arms and head until she fell back asleep. The sun peering through the curtain wakes me. The house is filled with the smell of fresh fried apples with cinnamon in the air. My phone rings and I scope the room out to make sure I'm alone before answering.

"Hello."

"Hello to you too."

I can tell by the voice that it's Meka.

"I had a wonderful time with you yesterday. You get me to do things I never imagined. I never expected to do some shit like that until I was married. So, with that being said…how do you see our future?"

"I'm not Miss Cleo so I can't see the future," I snapped.

"You know what I am talking about smart ass! I'm asking you… where do you see us or is it an us in your future? I don't want a sex partner I want a husband!"

"Listen here Miss Lady, it's too early for this shit and if you want a husband you need to go on a reality show."

"Bye… rude ass! Have a nice fucking day!"

Of course she finished by slamming the phone. The line went dead and I really didn't give a fuck. It was cool with me. I hopped out the bed and had me a serious stretch and yawn session. I slid my robe on and walked to the kitchen. Rhonda's definitely looking like my future wife. She's butt naked with an apron on preparing a great meal for her king. She's prepared fried apples, turkey bacon, French toast, the chicken fajita omelet, cran-apple Juice and milk.

"What are you waiting for? This food can't eat itself, you better dig in!"

Then my phone rings again, I flip it open thinking its Meka.

"What the fuck you want?"

Wrong! It's Mrs. Anderson.

"I beg your pardon? You need to watch that mouth of yours."

"I am sorry but people have been playing on my phone this morning, driving me crazy." I lied.

"Leave them monkeys alone and you won't have those types of problems. I set you up with a classy young lady who happens to be my baby sister, so know that the apple doesn't fall far from the tree... I am classy as they come. So have you talked to her?"

"Who?... your sister?" I asked out loud.

Chapter 9

Rhonda is standing in front of me waving me off as if she does not like her sister and doesn't want to be on the phone with her.

"No, I haven't talked to her since the other day I think, but on another note, we have this case in the bag."

"Oh I know we do! If you know like I do, the cake has been baked. I'll call you later to check on you. Oh … my sister says you were sick…you know I gave her a great recipe for homemade chicken soup. You should try to get you a bowl. I hope you get well soon."

"Thanks," I said.

For some reason I really appreciated that. You don't see too many people concerned with how the next person feels. Make sure you have a nice day and take care…bye.

I go back to eating and I ask Rhonda why she didn't want her sister to know that she was over here with me.

"Because I know how she is, she doesn't want to see me happy like she says she does. She is very judgmental and always has something negative to say about anybody I'm dealing with. She's always stressing me because she painted a picture like her relationship was flawless. Now you see he worked out for her ass. Now she sees how the other side feels."

"I feel you...sometimes people never take the time out to see if their roses really stink. "

I was caught off guard by how enraged Rhonda had become in a split second. I'm wondering where it was coming from. There's was a slight flame in Rhonda's eyes that said there was far more to the story than she was alluding. I want to know exactly what. I'm not going to press the issue until the opportunity presents itself. The once bubbly housewife in training now looks sad and distraught.

"Baby I will be right back."

She just nods as if to say yeah ok. I go into my bedroom and make a call.

"Yes, I would like to book a flight to Atlantic City? 2 tickets...yes, the earliest flight possible..."

After booking the reservations I hurried to prepare Rhonda for what's in store for her. When I walk up behind her she's drying the last of the dishes from this morning's breakfast. My manhood has already stiffened just from rubbing up against her. She surprised me last night. But, now that I know she's just as much a freak as I am it's on. I lean her over the kitchen counter and gently push her head into the sink. In less than a second I was on my knees tasting her sweet nectar from the back. As my tongue stroked both of her lips I can tell that it's working; her legs are going limp like noodles. I started by slowly darting my tongue in and out of her love tunnel. Then I sped up the pace until she couldn't take anymore. She came like crazy right on my face. I inserted my middle finger inside of her before placing that same finger in her mouth. At first she looked at me like I was crazy before willingly accepting my finger. She couldn't hide that she was turned out by the moment.

I scooped her into my arms carrying her into the shower. I washed her body using my hand as the washcloth. I took a mental picture of every part of her body. Her skin looks a little different on her left arm. I chalked it up to how the sleeves on her robe were rolled up while she did the dishes. She looked at me as if I was the man she'd been looking for her entire life. I got her now! She got a mischievous grin on her face. She pointed her tongue very sharply and led a small trail with it from my left earlobe down to the very tip of my shaft. The she darted her tongue in the hole.

"Ummm!" I moaned.

Rhonda began to lick slow circles around the mushroom. Then with an airtight grip she slowly descended on all 10 inches of this dick. She swallowed me so fast that I wasn't prepared. True story, I had to grab onto something to keep from falling out of the shower. Rhonda repeatedly teased me by licking slowly down the right side of the shaft, then back to the top. She repeated this process on the left side. The only difference this time was that when she got to the top, she lightly flicked the tip of her tongue across the tip of the rocket. Then sucked down so hard, like a vacuum, that she sucked the orgasm right out of me in no time. I watched in amazement as she swallowed every drop. Nothing escaped her mouth! She looked up and smiled at me knowing that she'd put her work in.

For a moment, I just looked into her eyes. My heart felt warm. Hold the fuck up, men don't feel warm! Now I'm feeling like a gump. I quickly snap out of it and grabs Rhonda's hand letting her know it's time to get out the shower. She follows me to the room to get dressed. Time slipped away so fast now we are behind schedule. I'm dressing and packing as fast as I could.

"C'mon on Rhonda baby… you are getting dressed too slow."

I grab my cell and call down to the lobby.

"Can you arrange for a car to pick my guest and I up in 15 minutes...oh and the destination is BWI airport…thanks we will be downstairs shortly. Please give me a call when they arrive."

"Wait one minute… what the hell is going on Felix? First you rush me to get dressed, then you order a car and you still haven't even taken the time to explain what the hell is going on."

"Sssshhhh baby…you got to trust me…"

I walk up and place and my fingers against her lips. Then I replace my finger with my mouth. I seductively devour her lips; making her forget about her questions.

"…I have a surprise for you honey. Let's go and don't worry about clothing either, I have you covered. Hey have you seen my cell? We have to go we're late."

"I will look for it now honey." Rhonda says.

I can tell she feels that my planning a surprise trip was the sweetest thing any man had ever done for her. She found the phone wrapped up in the comforter. Like clockwork it began to ring. Rhonda looked at the caller id and saw that the caller was calling from the building. She assumed it was the attendant calling to say the car had arrived to pick us up. Rhonda hits the answer button and before she can speak she hears:

"Papi… I'm waiting like a Spanish fly on the wall for you to dig deep inside me. When are you going to use your pass? Make me scream No Mas, Papi!"

I'm shitting bricks waiting on her reaction. I overheard every word! I guess because of the Spanish accent Rhonda assumed the person had the wrong number and I let her roll with that.

"I found your phone and...never mind… let's just go. I can't wait to spend some alone time with you today."

We kissed and headed downstairs for the car. Just as we got to the lobby floor I remembered something.

"Shit! I forgot something. Baby give me a sec."

"Ok baby …I will be waiting in the car."

I jumped back on the elevator. As soon as I walk off I walk right into Toya.

"Did you like what I said to you that much that you are back so soon? If so where is your coupon? Huh Papi?"

"Girl, those lips, those lips are gonna get you in trouble… There's nothing I'd love more than to stay and use my coupon…but I'm running late for a flight baby, I gotta go.

Toya is standing here in a silk see through butt length robe. Her body was calling for me to bite it. I may be slow but I ain't crazy, I got to think about the big picture. I concocted my next move and decided to play it safe. I'm not taking any chances, this time. I kissed her on her forehead and walked away thinking 'bout what she said about a call. I haven't talked to her. When did she call? By the time I turned around to ask her she was gone. I ran inside, grabbed my computer bag and ran back downstairs.

After a nice flight our plane lands and we walk through the terminal to the baggage claim. I notice that my Luis Vuitton luggage is gone and not rolling around this big ass circle. I'm getting mad as shit and frustrated that my things have not surfaced yet. Slowly but surely I begin to show my ass. I cut the fuck up so bad that this fake ass flash light security comes over like he is going to do something. What the fuck is he going to do, blind me with the light? They're telling me to calm down. I am looking at them like they are fucking crazy.

"How the hell is me calming down going to bring my shit back?"

"Boo forget it, don't let this ruin your evening and mini-vacation."

"You know what... you're so right babe. Maybe someone needs the stuff more than me and I know I can afford to replace anything that was lost. It's a small thing!! We'll just buy some things to wear while we are up here."

"Where are we headed anyway boo, you got me in the blind. But I am going to follow and let you lead."

We walked out of the airport and get into this nice ass 2010 pearl white Rolls Royce Phantom limo. The driver had two bottles of Ace of Spades champagne on ice, 3 long stem white roses, and a cold bowl of fresh fruit. So I popped the first bottle and we let champagne flow to get us buzzed. I asked the driver to take his time getting us to our destination. We are getting twisted! I am on the floor sucking on her toes. I'm licking up and down her thighs making her ocean overflow. It's starting to look like a tsunami with her juices running everywhere down her legs.

I start to feed her fresh grapes, pineapples, and strawberries dipped in chocolate. She's eating this shit up! I use my tongue to further drive her into a frenzy. She can't stay still! She's moaning and scratching on my body begging to jump on me but I'm not letting her. I'm enjoying teasing her to the point that she is ready to explode. Just as I was about to give in, we are pulling up to Homestead Restaurant. She's going to have to wait. This is one of the finest steak houses Atlantic City has to offer. We exit the limo tipsy, stumbling, and laughing loud just having a great time with each other.

I open the door for her and the hostess immediately greets us.

"Welcome to Homestead, and how are you this wonderful evening. Welcome to the home of the best steaks in Atlantic City, is this your first time visiting our pleasant establishment?"

"Yes," Rhonda answers.

The hostess escorts us to our private seating area. I pull out Rhonda's chair and she was shocked. She didn't even try to hide it all I could do was laugh to myself.

"Don't be surprised that there are some real men left out in the world," I tell her.

"I know that's right, haven't seen too many men that know about that nowadays," the lady sitting in a seat behind her shouts out.

I chuckle a little bit and Rhonda kicks me as if to say stop flirting with that bitch. Her face was clearly saying, *tell her to go find her own damn man.* Just to irritate her, I send the older lady a drink. Rhonda couldn't hide her jealousy.

"Keep playing with me if you want to!"

"Aww boo that's cute. I smell a little jealousy... but its okay because I am all yours."

"Yeah ok... you can play with me if you want." She said with her arms crossed and lips pouted.

I can tell she is catching feelings for me. This loving got her hooked. She's getting attached to me. The thought brings a smile to my face. The waiter comes to the table.

"What would you like to drink?"

"I'll have a bottle of red wine from the glass case behind the bar."

"Sir, those bottles start at 5."

"Okay...and?" I reply in an arrogant tone.

"Sir, I didn't mean anything by that."

"We must have one and you can bring that now... thanks!"

The way that he said the price gave the impression that we're here asking for a hand out or to wash dishes in the back. I just brushed it off. I've learned to take things with a grain of salt. Nothing is going to ruin the time I've planned on having with my future girl. The waiter comes back with the bottle in hand. He begins to pour. I tap the glass letting him know that's enough and begin to do a taste test. I swish the wine around in my mouth before giving him the ok to proceed. He pours each of us a glass and leaves the bottle on ice. He also leaves the basket of bread.

"Would you like to start off with a salad or appetizer this evening?" He asks.

"Yes, I'd like a Caesar Salad with grilled chicken and shrimp."

I really wanted to bust off on his ass because he was rubbing me the wrong way. But, the tight face that Rhonda was giving me calmed me down; so I played it cool. I ordered the same type of salad that Rhonda was having but with extra dressing, as well as a glass of ice water with lemon slices. We quickly got back on track. In no time flat, we are laughing and joking. She's rubbing her feet up and down my legs. She is really making my man stand at full attention. If she keeps going, this damn table is going to flip over. The waiter comes over with our order.

"Are you ready to order your entrees?"

Neither of us are really beef eaters but I order a Porter House steak well done with garlic potatoes, and steamed broccoli with melted cheese. Rhonda was like damn that sounds good so she ordered the same thing except that her steak was medium rare.

"They say the blood makes you horny," she says.

"What are you a vampire?" I asked.

My ass was thinking something totally different. To me that blood shit makes you crazy! I didn't want to ruin her lil' moment so I kept my thoughts to myself. We enjoyed our meal and conversation. I learned a lot about her. The time flew by. As the night went on, I started thinking to myself that she might really be the one. We talked about our past, future, and everything in between. I laughed to myself. Damn she's good! She has me, me of all people, openly and happily talking about my future.

I've been flip flopping between the same women for over a year now and none of them could pay me to talk about my future, especially with them. I had to give her the props she deserved.

"You are damn good sweetheart, you know that?" I say.

"Honey what are you talking about?" she asks.

"Nothing baby...nothing at all."

"Would you all like to order any dessert?" the waiter asks.

"Would you like some dessert honey?" I asked

Rhonda's expression clearly showed that she was stuffed. Her eyes said hell no! I took the hint.

"No thank you... we will just take the bill please"

I can't help staring at Rhonda's taut nipples. They are standing at full attention. They look like a World War 3 drill sergeant, preparing for a sneak attack. My thoughts of those pretty nipples in my mouth made me laugh to myself. I pictured my hands on an excavation mission traveling south on her body. I know that drilling inside her oil well will bring me nothing but riches and pleasure. The maitre de brought out the bill and lays it face down on the table. Rhonda licks her lips as though she envisioning being under the table with her tongue salsa dancing on both of my inner thighs until I just can't take it anymore.

"You look like you trying to do a lil' something?"

"What the hell?" I said holding the bill.

"What's wrong with the bill baby?"

"They must've made a technical error. When they said 5 I didn't think that it would have that many zeros behind it!"

"Well how many zeros did they add?"

"I think they made a mistake on this bill, this mu'fucka say $5,000.00. Either they made a mistake or gave us the wrong check. I could've sworn it was just two people sitting at this table. The bill equals two mortgages and your car notes and mine put together to the 4th power."

"What the hell does that equal?"

"You should know, your ass is in school."

"Well will it be a problem to pay the bill... like this is so damn embarrassing. Do you have it or not? I mean...I can help you out but you chose this place so I thought you knew what was going on in this "establishment"?"

I just look at Rhonda with a smirk on my face. She obviously was not finding my joke funny in the least bit. All of this feistiness' and new found aggression she was exhibiting was making my dick grow larger and larger by the second.

"Hello, snap the hell out of it, are you here with me right now."

All I could do was laugh to myself. I decided to go further with the joke.

"We got to options, we could A) Run outta this mu'fucka or B) I could pay for this mu'fucka and be homeless?''

"I think we will take option b!" Rhonda snaps in a sassy tone.

She was letting me know that she didn't find this shit to be funny. I was laughing so hard I was about to pee on myself.

"Awww man...I thought you was a rider. You're supposed to say option A," I joked.

I can see that she's really not finding my jokes to be funny.

"I was just kidding."

I whip out the Centennial Card aka the BLACK CARD and hand it to the maitre de. The maitre de returns with the receipt. I sign it and we get up to leave. The waiter is hanging around obviously waiting for a tip.

"Shiiit you better get your tip out that 5 thousand," I say before I burst out laughing."

We walk out of that high ass restaurant, the limo driver opens the door and we get in.

"I will never come back to this place ever again," Rhonda declares.

"Why you say that?"

"Not in my wildest dreams did I ever think a dinner bill would be the price of a used car. The food was good but not that damn good! I would have been better off if you took me to a fast food place. You know all that fancy shit does nothing for me."

But little does she know, her talking like that is turning me on to the fullest extent. I got me a woman who would choose a Big Mac over a lobster. Then on top of that she got her own dough. She's going on and on to the point, I just want her to shut up by slamming this musket in her mouth. Or, I can just dig into her ribs until she can't say a word. Finally, the Phantom pulled into the circular driveway in front of the Borgata Hotel. This hotel is the only casino/hotel that can compare to the ones in Vegas. They just added another area in the hotel called The Water Club, which is so damn sexy. When we get out the bell hop leads us through the lobby area to the front desk where we will be checking in. As we walk up, I notice my long time friend from around the way. She moved up here to change her life. I see she's still working here so I have to say wassup. So we begin a friendly conversation.

"I haven't seen you up here in minute. Are you using your club Black Card today?"

She already knew the answer but I played along just to entertain her.

"Yes I will be, so make sure you hook me up. We have to go shopping since somebody stole my luggage."

"Well you know I got you… this must be the one right here Felix! She must be some kind of special because you never bring anyone up here with you. She's cute…she looks real familiar though. She looks like this young lady that used to come around you know who when I was living down there out in that other life."

I'm thinking to myself, is this woman on America's Most Wanted or something? Everybody seems as if they've seen this girl before. This shit got me a little puzzled. All that really matters is that I'm digging her or at least that's what I'm going to keep telling myself. We gather ourselves and go up to our room so she can rest and freshen up.

Chapter 10

While Rhonda is napping, I go downstairs to gamble and shop. The first place I stop is the Hugo Boss store to snatch me up some shirts, shoes, and pants. Since Rhonda loves rocking sunglasses and I love my lady to look nice, I grab a pair of shades for her as well. The way I see it, if you got money to spend, then spend it. Making my way through the shops, something catches my eye. It was this tight Roberto Cavalli bag that Rhonda would look great with. I walk in the store and looked around to see if there was something else that Rhonda would look sexy in or with. It's not like I am spending my money anyway. This is the money that was leftover from the winnings. I knew that I would be back, so I had them put my winnings on my Borgata Black Card. This way when I returned I could live it up and be proud of myself. Yeah, I'm a real slick one.

While browsing I hear a familiar voice. It sounds like Nikki. I turn around to face the voice but no one was there. I know Nikki's voice when I hear it and that was Nikki. I'm positive. As many years as I have been dealing with that woman I can't forget her voice. There it is again. I still don't see anyone.

Maybe I miss her so much that I am tripping! I know one way to fix this so I text her. Just like the other day, Nikki didn't respond and probably didn't really give a fuck about me trying to reach her. I began questioning why I said what I said to her. As I was putting my phone back into the holster, my text message alert went off. I smiled thinking that it was Nikki but I was wrong; it was Toya sending me some naked pictures. It was like 6 of them. She was doing different poses and using different objects. The first picture, she stuck a TV remote control in her vagina. The second picture she is sitting on a bathroom plunger. And, goodness gracious, the third one! The third one was a video where she made her pussy drink water and squirts it all out. I had to check my pants to make sure the gun didn't fire in my jeans and cause a scene. I scroll down to the message.

"I stopped dancing completely and I'm all yours now."

I flashed back to when I told her if she ever stopped stripping she would be my wife. Man, I am up here with Rhonda talking 'bout our future; I'm hearing Nikki's voice, Meka on some bullshit! Man, this is too much! My brain can't function. The phone rings again. This time it's Mrs. Anderson. I took a minute contemplating whether or not to answer it. While trying to decide, my fingers slip and accidentally hit talk.

"Hello," she says.

"Hello Mrs. Anderson, how are you doing today?"

"I pray you didn't forget that we have a big event on our schedule. I am worried because I have not heard from you." Mrs. Anderson says after clearing her throat.

"Yes I know, and I am ready for it. I have no choice but to attack it head on and be ready."

"Ok... I'm just making sure my sister didn't get you side tracked because this is more important than her...

I looked at the phone in disgust not believing that she just said that. I am so stunned that I have to take a second and pause.

"...Did you hear me? I know how my sister can be a pest and a fuck up and I don't need anyone to stand in the way of what is rightfully mine. You catch my drift?"

"Yes I understand fully and I am on top of it. I won't let you down."

"Make sure you enjoy the rest of your day,"

I began to walk to the elevator and my mind's playing tricks on me. I could've sworn that I saw someone that looked just like Nikki getting off the elevator across from me. The doors on my elevator closed so fast I didn't get a good look. When I entered my room, the lights were dim, Sensual Amber blessed the air, and Rhonda was lying in the middle of the bed with rose petals around her in a heart shape. There was one petal on each nipple and a group that covered her goodies. There was a bowl laying beside her right hip on the bed with whipped cream, chocolate syrup, cherries, nuts, handcuffs, feathers, sex dice, and a blind fold. Later for the blindfolds, I want to see.

The first thing I do is make a human sundae by pouring Hershey syrup on her thighs. I spray the whipped cream on each nipple and down to her belly button. I sat a cherry on top of each area then prepare to sprinkle some...naw as a matter of fact, I have my own nuts for this occasion. I began to eat and nibble every section one spot at a time. Now that's she's juicy and ready, I put the blind fold on her and handcuffed her to the bed posts. I shook the dice in my hand and rolled it on the bed beside her. The dice bumped against her soft skin landing on *"kiss below the waist"*. I follow instructions well, so I go down and start to tongue kiss her clit. The ecstasy is driving her crazy. Next, I put her legs in the air and ran the feather down her legs tickling her butt. She's bucking like a wild horse. I played near her other hole with the feather and then watched her cum against her will. I licked her butt next and she went numb. I rolled the dice again as I teased her butt hole sensually with the feather. I know she's ready to really explode. The dice read, "*blow in ear*". As I was blowing in her ear, I can tell she's completely surrendered herself to me. I got to saying some of the freakiest shit she has ever heard in her life.

"You want Daddy to kiss you from your head to your toes?"

"Yes please," she purred.

I put some ice chips in my mouth and began to kiss her, sending a chill up your spine. Her knees began to shake.

"You want some more?"

"Oh yes baby, yes?"

"Tell Daddy you want this dick."

"I want it Daddy...I want it so bad."

I opened her legs and slid right into her waterfall. I was stroking so good her left rib was getting touched on the regular. With each stroke I got thicker. I'm beginning to fill her hole; it's going to be sore in the morning. My objective is to have her walking pigeon toed when I finish. I want to hear her say that I messed up her bladder. So we going at it and I'm starting to sweat. That's when you know you are putting in work. Rhonda is clawing into my back. She's begging me to go deeper. She's on the verge of an orgasm that is going to have her body locked like an engine with no oil. I am about to explode with her at the same time. We're in perfect unison. She can feel my manhood jump and I can feel her

Harlem shake until the last drop. Got damn! That was some good shit.

We laid there for a few minutes basking in all our glory. We began to have a heart to heart talk about where we see this going between us. For real, after a nut like that I just want to go to sleep. But, she wants to discuss how we're not getting any younger. I play along.

"I am not looking for a sex partner. I'm looking for someone who is in it for the long haul. I want the dream. A real family and the home with the white picket fence! You know…kids and a husband, the whole fairy tale. If that's not something you want, just tell me… and I promise I won't be mad. I know that you didn't force me to fall for you."

"To be quite honest, I thought I wanted to chase women forever… but I see that's getting boring. I guess too many feelings are involved. At the end of the day, it seems like I don't care when I really do. My way of showing it is just a little different than others. That lifestyle has become a headache with this girl on Monday and this girl on Tuesday. Plus my mother keeps pressing me for some grand kids so it might be time. And you seem like someone I can grow old with. So far you have earned my trust."

"I have something to tell you Felix…"

Then there is a knock at the door.

"Who is it?"

The voice says that they have a delivery for Rhonda. Rhonda looks at me for approval. I nod my head so she put her robe on, and opens the door. From the angle I was laying, I could see her big mouth wide open. Her jaw line was practically dragging the floor. There the bell hop stood outside the door holding a big red shiny Roberto Cavalli in one hand. And, a Louis Vuitton dog bag complete with cutest little brown and black Yorkie in the other. She just stood there crying. She was so emotional I had to get up and go get the stuff from the bell hop.

"Nobody has ever treated me like I was special before. Nobody ever really cared about me."

"What were you going to tell me earlier?"

She's so wrapped up into the damn dog that she was not even paying me any attention. I left it alone and just made a mental note to ask her later. I jumped in the shower and made it my business to get red carpet fresh for us to go to the boardwalk shops and then gamble. When I get out the shower, I glance over at Rhonda and she looks happy as ever. She's playing with the dog like it was a newborn baby. I can't seem to shake what her sister said earlier. I really want to tell baby girl, but she is in such a good mood and I don't wanna ruin that for her. I dried off and got laced with my new shit. I put on a nice black three button Gucci top, some Gucci ashy denim jeans, and a pair of black Gucci tennis shoes. Your boy was Gucci from head to toe! The cologne was on a million too! Put it this way, I looked better than a runway model. I am red carpet fresh; ready for my interview with Joan Rivers.

While I finish prepping myself, Miss Lady is on her way into the shower. I grab her by the arms and kiss her like she has never been kissed before. I glanced at her arms. It's marked up. Maybe the dog scratched her or she is a diabetic or something. Again, I brush it off and she goes off to wash her ass. Eventually she gets dressed. She looks good enough to eat. As Jody says, she has on this sexy blue "all purpose dress". This joint is hugging every curve on her body, and believe me, she has a lot of those. It looks painted on.

It's time to paint the city red! Time to shut it down like I always do! We take the elevator and go downstairs. Then we take the ride over to the boardwalk shops and mall to spend a little dough. I want her to really enjoy our out of town mini-vacation. We're shopping to get something fresh, slick, and sexy for the Maxwell Concert tomorrow night. She doesn't even know that I bought the tickets. As we take the ride over there my text messages go off.

Rhonda has my phone, so while she was passing my G1 over to me; she was reading the text. She got this funky look on her face. When she hands me the phone, I scroll down and see that the message is from her sister.

"Don't forget what we talked about!"

I don't know what Rhonda actually saw or read. When we pull up in front of the shops, she is asking questions.

"Why is my sister texting you and what the hell does she mean? What is she referring to?"

"Most likely the case, that's what we talk about," I responded calmly.

"My sister is so jealous of me that I know she would say anything to destroy my happiness. She only introduced me to you so she can tear us apart and talk shit about me; like she always does… because my life is a game to her. So at the end of the day, my pain and heartache is her excitement," She explains through her tears.

"Boo forget her, this is our day. The devil is always working…make sure you remember that what God has for you,

NO ONE can destroy it. We will not let anyone rain on our parade."

"OK... baby, I got you."

She took a few minutes to get herself together. My phone begins to ring and its Meka. You know damn well I'm not going to answer it so I sent her ass straight to voicemail. Normally, she would never leave a message but this time the new message icon popped up on my screen. I excused myself, dialed my number to check the voicemail, and listened to Meka talking slick out her damn mouth.

"You think your ass is so motherfucking slick huh? So I guess you up in Atlantic City with your sister huh? You are a fast talking son of a bitch that's what you are nigga. I just got a picture of you and your bitch kissing and holding hands. I just might come up there and fuck you and her up. I knew if you would've answered that you would've lied like a punk ass bitch! Lose my fucking number jerk!"

I'm sitting here with the stuck face looking stupid as hell! Rhonda wants to know if everything is ok. I tell her I'm cool and that I just have something on my mind. What I am really trying to figure out is who would do some bamma shit like that? I am trying to run through my brain everybody who has seen me or that I saw that could be suspect in this case. I thought I saw Meka's brother, wit' his police ass, but I turned my back on him so I wouldn't stare. I tell you one thing, if it is him, I am going to smack this shit out his police ass. There is just certain shit within the "real man society" that you just do not do; **under any circumstances**. My phone rings and breaks my train of thought.

"Hello what it do my nig?" I say.

"What's good son? Where you at playboy?" Rick asks.

"I'm up in Atlantic City at our spot… doing what we do best."

That's when Rick dogged me and told me I was some shit for not letting him know that I was coming up top. I tried to explain to him that it was a spur of the moment trip. I was taking Rhonda to make her feel better. He definitely was not having that shit.

"I have to see this bitch…I mean, chick my bad, you keep talking 'bout because you are breaking all your own rules. You never trick nigga. What the hell is going on? She must have some bomb, bomb, bomb ass pussy for you to be tricking like that. You probably 'bout to wife her ass too aren't you?

You know I didn't respond.

"… I knew it nigga you thinking way to damn hard and haven't answered me yet. Your pressed ass probably has picked out a ring and every fucking thing. You supposed to be my manz what the hell? You probably tongue kissed her, put your tongue in her ass and some more shit. Awww man dawg."

"Hell yeah I kissed her and ate her ass! I'm tricking so what nigga? We are not kids any damn more. Oh and yeah… I'm claiming her as my girl, I go with her so now what!"

Rick was dying laughing on the phone. He made me feel like a fucking clown. I just hung up the phone and put it back in my pocket. Rick called right back.

"Alright man, I see you're in your feelings about this chick. I just wanna know if you have talked to Nikki?"

"Not right now man…come on man!"

"Naw... I just thought about something...for real this time. Have you talked to Nikki? Cause it is mighty funny that you are up A.C. at the same time that she is. Ya'll up there at the same exact time and you are not together? What type of shit are ya'll two on? She's up there with her lil friend and you up there with your lil friend! Ya'll doing it!" Rick is cracking up laughing."

I can tell that Rick is in tears now by how hard he is laughing. He's hysterical.

"Who is she up here with? Is it the one you gave the head to on the first date?"

Now it's my turn to laugh. Rick isn't finding that shit funny 'cause he didn't think that I knew he was breaking all the rules.

"You are so funny man. She's up there with her lil male friend..."

Total silence was in the air.

"...I knew you wouldn't find that shit funny nigga. Now what... the cat got your tongue huh? Where your jokes at now?" Rick teased.

I was so mad I just hung the phone up. The dial tone was all he heard. I began apologizing to Rhonda for being rude and talking loud. We were having a wonderful time, walking along side the water on the boardwalk. To cover up my mistake we walked into Juicy Couture. I felt I should get her something for treating her like she was not here and for catching feelings with Rick over the fact that Nikki is here with another nigga. The whole time I am thinking about how fast Nikki is moving on. l I start to feel bad. I peeped her noticing the necklace, ring, and bracelet set, so I got that for her. Then we headed to the Gucci store. It's a must that I cop me some shoes every time I come up here. I forgot that the pretty young lady that I am up here with is not what I am used to. Rhonda is pretty wealthy herself! I'm out her stuntin' and shopping, I am copping everything that I see her look at when she thinks I am not looking. Her money might be longer than mines but I can tell that she saves. I'm flossing and tricking my dough on her like it's nothing!

As soon as we hit the Gucci store, my eyes zoom in on the new Gucci driver shoes. I have been dying for these joints! They had them available in both white and black so I HAD to get both. The total for them both was about $800; even so I wasn't even close to the limit that I planned on not going over. Then, I grabbed me a pair of Velcro Sneakers with signature web for $475, the bi-fold wallet with the Gucci strip logo tag for $245, a solid black silk tie, and a diagonal strip tie with the Gucci script logo. At this point, I'm losing count. I know I have room to play in here, but I go to the counter anyway to cash out. As the cashier is ringing up my belongings, I am showing Rhonda my choices. She is telling my how cute each item is and how she's gonna dress in nothing but a tie and wait for me in bed. I am so into what she's saying, I didn't notice that my man was standing up like a rocket. She looks down at me with a seductive smile. I know why so I turn away from the counter for a sec to get myself together. While I am counting my money to get ready to pay, I hear the salesman:"Thank you ...come again soon."

Chapter 11

Now, I am a little confused. I don't even care that my man is knocking down shelves; I have to turn around and see what the hell is going on. Before I could ask what was going on, Rhonda looked at me and said that she had taken care of it. I had this look on my face like, Daaamn! I did forget that shorty got just as much as me in the bank, if not more. She walked up to me, kissed me on my cheek, and laughed as she walked out of the door leaving me standing there in awe by myself. Lord knows I am not used to a woman who can pay for my shopping urges.

"Come again. You have a wonderful woman, you don't find them too often!" the salesman says as he walks away.

A million things are running through my mind. I can't stop smiling. I felt like a kid in the candy store. As I walked outside Gucci bags in hand, I feel like a million bucks. Rhonda started to sing.

"Anything you can do… I can do better…"

I couldn't help but to laugh at how happy it seems to make her by pleasing me. All I could think at this point is that I have never been out stunted. She must've been reading my mind.

"It's a first time for everything…"

I was taken aback. Is she reading my mind or what? We continued to shop and tore up the stores together; just splurging on one another. I have one more trick up my sleeve for her though; especially since I know what she is used to now. I thought outside the box, trying to make her have a mental orgasm. I wanted to push it to the extreme. It's easy to sex a woman and make her cum, but it takes some skill to make her brain have a orgasm. I'm out to make her cry. Then I can catch that tear on her cheek, lick it off, and kiss her with it still on my tongue. I bet she gets a chill beyond her wildest dream. I have her mind going on right now. We are on our way back to the hotel. It's only 8:00 and to me that is too early to turn in. I asked the driver to make the right towards this private air field instead of making a left.

We pull up to the red carpet on the runway of the heliport. We hop over to the Big Apple to see Oprah's Broadway play, "Color Purple" starring Fantasia Barrino. Once we arrive in New York City about 45 minutes later. One of my attorney buddies that I went to school with had arranged for a limo to be waiting for us when we landed.

"Where are we headed? You didn't tell me we were going anywhere else. I didn't have a chance to freshen up."

"Shhhhh…Rhonda, I got you! Boo you look good! I would never set you up and put you in a fucked up situation trust me."

The limo navigates its way across town. It's New York so you know there's more than a little traffic. The show starts in about 45 minutes, the limo driver assures us that we will arrive on time if it's the last thing he does. After he rolls up the privacy screen, Rhonda immediately begins to unzip my pants. She begins to play the trombone like she was in the Howard U. marching band. Suddenly she stops.

"Why did you stop?"

"I'm playing follow the leader. Whatever the driver does, I'm going to do. If he drives fast, I go fast. If he drives slowly, I slow it down. Do you follow me?"

I nod my head yes. True to her word she follows the motion for motion. I was almost at the point where my tire was going to lose air, and she stop again. I was so blown that she'd stopped again. The driver announced over the speaker that we'd arrived at the venue. Me being the freaky dude that I am, I was tempted to tell the driver to circle the block but I didn't want to mess the mood up. We go inside and had seats right next to a couple of entertainers. My VIP swag is on a hundred. About 45 minutes into the play it gets very interesting. They remade the movie to a T. I feel a hand slid under mines. For a second, we're looking like a couple. It feels kinda cool. It's definitely something I'm not used to. The play is coming to an end. We start to exit trying to beat everybody else to the lobby. I want to buy a few souvenirs for my mother. It's bad enough I came without her and brought another woman. But, if I don't bring her anything back she is definitely going to act a fool, loose her religion, and curse my ass out. The phone rings and this time it isn't mines, its Rhonda's. Whoever is on the phone is questioning her like the police. Who is she with? Where is she? Why?

I hear her telling them where she is and who she was with. The next thing I hear is somebody yelling to their top of the lungs. Suddenly, she starts crying and running as fast as she can out the front door. Me being me, I chase behind her trying to find out what's wrong. She is really letting the tears fall. I ask her if everything is good but she keeps hunching her shoulders. She's telling me she doesn't want to talk about it or involve me with her family business.

"That's understandable...much respect here. When you feel ready to talk about it, let me know."

Ten minutes go pass and she lashes out beginning to vent.

"How dare that bitch tell me if you lose the case she is going to kill me? She says that if it wasn't for her... I would be broke in the slums or dead somewhere. And, that I'm never going to amount to shit. Like... the nerve of this bitch. She acts like I wasn't left the same amount of money when my parents died. For some reason, her brain makes her really think that she's better than me. She is nowhere near my level! Yes, I had a few setbacks but that's why I'm in school and in church so heavily. The devil can stay away from the anointed. This is real talk Felix... like you are the only person in my corner. It's like my family likes me better when I'm at the bottom but I'm not going to go back down. I will remain a fighter to get to the ultimate goal."

I grab her into my arms and let her cry it out on my shoulder. I'm starting to think that I could get used to this. I like making her feel better. Not to mention, it sure as hell does feel good waking up beside her in the morning.

"Baby come on... let's go get in the car."

We get into the limo and ride directly to the Borgata. I tipped the driver $300 to show my appreciation. I can tell that Rhonda's tired so I carry her to the elevator and all the way to our room. I undress her, put on her silk night gown, and tuck her into bed. I take a seat in this obviously expensive chair and begin to rub my eyes reflecting on the events of past few weeks. I have lost both Meka and Nikki. Nikki actually could have been the one; but I just wasn't ready. When Rhonda rolls over I realize that I'm talking to myself aloud. I kiss her on the forehead, shower, and decide to go gamble.

Downstairs in the lobby, the Borgata Babes are really encouraging me by enticing me to buy these damn drinks. I'm at the crap table getting it in! I'm winning so much money from the cum out and my favorite numbers 6, 8, and 9. I'm doubling down every single time. I'm up about 15 grand. I'm about to call it quits 'cause the nigga that's about to roll looks like a bitch when My Borgata Babe brings me a drink that I didn't order.

"Thanks but I didn't order this drink. I'mma take it anyway though…I knew your sexy ass was diggin the kid," I said arrogantly.

The Borgata Babe sizes me up; undressing me with her eyes.

"Actually this drink is from the young lady over there."

She points towards the Black Jack table. I don't know that woman. She's sitting with her back to me so I can't see her face. From the back she's rocking a sexy ass short hair cut that's making my dick rise faster than your chances at losing the Powerball. Down boy! I walk over to the table and my mouth dropped to the floor. Standing in front of me is Nikki. Not the Nikki I'm used to, this is like Nikki 2.0. She's on some new shit!

"Shit, got damn!"

I grabbed Nikki and went to hug her and kiss them sexy ass lips that were wet with lip gloss. Nikki pushed me away as if to say this ain't yours anymore.

"Oh… I'm sorry I just have missed you so much. I have been texting you. Then I get a call that you're up here with some bama ass nigga. I see you have the Halle Berry thing going on. I don't even know what to think right now."

Nikki was looking at me like I'm a bitch! I read her mind. I can't believe I'm standing here looking like a damn fool pouring my heart out to this girl and she bout to carry me. Naw fuck this I'm about to just be out of here. But I can't just walk away from her, I think I love her and her son and he isn't even mine. Man what am I going to do? My thoughts are running 300 mph and I can't stop pondering what to do next? Fuck this, I am a man, no I am THE MAN! I lean into Nikki so fast that she didn't have time to show her disgust. I begin to kiss her with more passion than I have ever kissed Rhonda with. The look on Nikki's face coupled with the tears in her eyes told that she missed me. Her kiss said that she thought she was over me but she loves me more than I love myself. I look into her eyes and with as much sincerity as I could muster I said:

"Baby... I am so sorry that I hurt you and I will never do anything other than make you feel like the queen you are."

Nikki wrapped her arms around my neck.

"I love you Felix Joseph Williams."

I looked into her eyes and said that I loved her back. That was all Nikki had ever really wanted.

"Can I order a Grey Goose and Cranberry?"

While all of this is going on, Rhonda has apparently awaken from her nightmares and decided to shoot some dice at the Crap Table. Unbeknownst to me, she threw on her Baby Phat Velour sweat suit that is making her ass fuller than Janice Dickerson from America's Next Top Model's lips and skipped her ass down to the casino. Apparently she'd walked around to all the craps tables looking for me. She ordered a drink and sat at a slot machine. The Borgata babe returns with the drink, accepts the tip, licks her lips at Rhonda and then walks off. A crowd had gathered around Nikki and I, and I guess the applause caught her attention. She turns around to see what's going on. The applause and whistles were getting louder as she walked towards the crowd.

"What is going on?"

"Some long lost couple that was on the outs just rekindled their flame."

She cut through the crowd, and found me down on one knee proposing to some woman she didn't even know existed. Either the event or the size of the rock knocked her off her feet, literally.

I have no idea that her eyes are stinging as she just stands there with tears running down her face. As the crowd disperses, she watches me carry this estranged woman away to the elevator. However, she manages to snap a picture of the woman's face and one of us together looking like we have been living in bliss for years. I know she was tempted to run after me but I guess she didn't want to risk embarrassing herself. She knew that I wasn't crazy enough to bring the woman back to our room so she hurried into another elevator and rushed to pack her bags. She calls a cab and leaves a note for Felix on the nightstand. The note was messy. I guess she can barely write because her eyes are burning so bad from crying and not really wanting to do what she knew she was about to do. The letter was short and to the point.

"Felix sorry about the quick getaway I am about to make, but I have class tomorrow. I will call you when I get the chance. I hope you will understand and continue to enjoy your trip. Thanks for everything; I really needed this eye opening trip!"

Love,

Rhonda

I can't believe what had just happened. I fucked this all the way up. I'm scared out of my mind. What am I going to say to Rhonda? Nikki was here with her son's father and I was here with Rhonda. I have been making love to Nikki all night. It is now after sunrise and I woke up next to my new fiancé in our NEW room. We made love like newlyweds and talked about how things were going to change. It was like I fell in love with Nikki all over again. Then all of a sudden, reality kicked in and I realized that haven't talked to or heard from Rhonda. Nikki noticed me moving around and figured that I was about to leave.

"Baby I have to go; the room is paid for so relax as much as you need. I have to get back to town to work on this case. I told you that I didn't plan on staying and they lost my luggage and…anyway I have paid for the room so relax yourself," I explained in a rush.

Then I remembered something, she was up here with her sucker ass baby-father, Chris. When the hell did he get back into the picture? His ass has been locked up since Nikki was pregnant and they were just friends.

"I want you to know that whatever you want me to do… I am willing to do. I know I am up here with…you know who. But it's nothing! We are not together, it's just that I was lonely and he was there and…" she couldn't even figure out the rest of the words.

"Listen, I want you to stay here for a couple of days and relax. I will make arrangements for us to move when I get back. Just relax and I am going to take care of you right this time! This I promise."

Nikki just looked in disbelief. She had no choice but to just nod her head and lay back down. I began to dress in a hurry. All types of thoughts are running through my head. What is Rhonda going to think? Is she worried? What the hell am I gonna say? Nikki notices the confusion on my face and tells me that it will be alright. I leave out heading to the room I shared with Rhonda.

I caught the elevator down to the 1st floor to where Rhonda and I were booked. I hesitated before entering because I still don't know what I'm going to say. The only thing I do know is that I fucked up. I actually bought the engagement ring from Ultimate Diamonds for Rhonda because she is who I thought I wanted. Now I don't know who I want. I was missing Nikki something terrible but I had no idea that it was to the point where I wanted to really marry her. She wanted to marry me, not the other way around. She does make me happy so I guess that's enough. But then what about Rhonda? This has been the best time that I've ever had with any woman. But, Nikki has earned her keep. I was just being afraid of commitment, right? But, Rhonda showed me what it feels like to wake up to the same woman everyday and I was just jive loving it! I opened the door and I got the shock of my life. Rhonda was gone! The bed was made, room empty, and Rhonda was nowhere to be found. You could tell that housekeeping had cleaned the room spotless. I didn't even know what to think. The only thing that was running through my mind was that Rhonda had to have seen me. But how?

When my nerves finally began to settle down, I noticed a letter on the night stand. After reading the letter I felt a little bit better. I decided to call Rhonda's cell phone and it went straight to voicemail. I tried several more times only to get the same result.

My head's spinning! I'm so confused! I plopped down onto the bed and waited for Rhonda to call or, at least that's what I told myself.

"Shit," I yelled to the top of my lungs.

Several hours passed by. I was sleeping so good that I awoke to 11 missed calls. The voicemail buzzing on my cell phone snapped me back to reality. I opened my eyes and looked at the clock. Damn, I slept until 3:00. I looked at the phone and erased the voicemail icon so I can see who has called. Nobody that I wanted to talk to had called, or maybe it was just because Rhonda had not called. It was the usual my mom, the office, Mrs. Anderson, Rick, and Nikki like a thousand times. All I could do was laugh to myself at how I've been behaving. I put myself in the predicament that I'm in now. Part of me was actually elated that Rhonda was not in the room because even right now I still did not know what I was going to say. How can I explain why I left the room and had not returned until the following morning?

I really do feel bad. But, seeing Nikki with that short hair cut did something to me. I was drunk as hell; I got caught up. She was sending me drinks. That shit really turned me on in a way that was ridiculous. On top of that, I was missing her way more than I would've ever expected. I ain't gonna lie, I even missed her son. I thought I didn't even want kids. Fuck this, I need to get back to the city so I can work on the case before I fuck around and lose my damn job! Hell, I am already losing my damn mind! I laughed to myself. I placed a call down to the front desk and had them call a car to take me to the airport. It's time to get home and back to work. Right after I made the call my phone buzzed. I answered it so fast you could tell I was pressed but I was expecting it to be Rhonda.

Chapter 12

"Hey baby where are you? Hello, are you there?" I asked.

"Damn… I didn't know you missed me that much since I hadn't heard from you since you left me the other day?" Toya said softly.

I was so blown that it was not Rhonda that I just want to hang up.

"I have a surprise for you when you get home Papi! See you sooner than later hopefully!"

She hung up before I could respond. I really didn't even have the energy to argue or try to figure out what she meant. Between all the sex I'm having lately and the predicament that I'm in, I'm exhausted. I plan on sleeping the entire 30 minute flight back home. I really feel bad about the situation I'm in but I have no answers on how to get out of this mess. Then it dawned on me to call Mrs. Anderson and see if she's spoken to Rhonda.

"Good morning Mrs. Anderson. I hope that all is well. I am on my way back into town to finish up with this case, but I just wanted to ask if you have talked to your sister?"

"No I have not, but why do you ask? I thought you called me to give me good news about the case. And as far as I am concerned she is NOT one of my concerns especially right now.

4 Play

And if you let her get in the way of my billion dollar divorce case, the both of you will be dealt with. Do you understand me? I tried to explain myself to you the other day, now if Rhonda is making you lose focus, I can either have you taken off the case or get rid of her, which would you prefer?..."

I was so shocked at what she was saying that I didn't have the faintest idea of what the answer should be. Or get rid of her? Mrs. Anderson is coming off like she's a gangster or something! What the hell was that supposed to mean?

"...ARE WE CLEAR GOT DAMMIT? I will let nothing and no one get in the way of what is mine!" She yelled.

Just like that, she hung up the phone. She didn't even let me respond. I'm so exhausted I don't even care. I'm sitting in the airport feeling like the dirtiest dude on earth. I closed my eyes and rested until the ride to the airport was over. I finally boarded the plane and shortly thereafter was home in D.C. During the car ride from the airport to my penthouse loft I slept like a baby. When I walked in the building, Timmy gave me this look of surprise.

"Why didn't you tell me you were ordering furniture and rearranging your suite? You sure do move fast," Timmy yelled as I was getting on the elevator.

I looked at him like he was crazy. The ride to the loft seemed like an eternity. I tried to figure out what the hell Timmy was talking about? I opened the door and had to do a double take. I had to make sure that I was in the correct loft. This shit is completely different. I don't know what the hell is going on. I slowly walked in further. I can smell something that's making my stomach growl. Then I had to take a step back. Who the hell is in here? I tip toed like a punk to the kitchen where the smell was emanating from. There she is, Toya lying on my kitchen island butt ass naked. She

111

has delicacies covering her most intimate areas. She looks delectable but how the fuck did she get in? And, where the hell is my furniture? I paused for a second because I didn't know whether to feast or be afraid of what the hell was happening here. My "lil big man" made me start to walk towards her, and then I stopped abruptly because I felt violated. I cleared my throat.

"Listen, you are looking really delicious over there but we can't do this shit right now."

"You don't really mean that you are just having a bad day, so come over here and let me make you feel better," she says completely ignoring my apparent irritation with her very uninvited presence.

I mean mug her so she knows that I am serious. She gets up and allows the food to roll onto the hardwood floor. She walks over and grabs my dick thinking it will change my mind.

"Get the fuck off of me and get outta here. I am not playing with you girl. I have never hit a woman but your ass is pushing it. Where the fuck is all of my shit? Did you steal my key? How the fuck did you get in here? Just leave before you make me say some shit I may regret for real…"

I scream while guiding her obsessed ass to the door at the same time. I'm so fatigued! At this point, I just want this bitch out of my loft so I can rest. Toya just stood there and looked at me with a face full of confusion. She doesn't even know what she should say.

"…Fine since you're a little slow, let me say it again. I want you to get the fuck out. I will give you some time to get your shit together and get this shit out of my got damn house before I get back."

112

As I'm walking to the elevator and phone begins to ring and its Meka.

"I know you weren't going to act like a skirt and not pick your phone up to call me, if so that's some sucker shit to do."

"See that's your problem your damn mouth is going to get you in trouble. What did you want me to call and say? The last thing I remember, you were threatening me, talking big shit, then you hung up. At this point in my life, I'm just trying to be successful and happy; with no damn stress. I don't want any problems! We all make mistakes trying our hands; you know testing the water, to see if it's something better out here when we already have the best."

"So what you're really trying to say boy is that I'm the best thing for you? Wait don't answer that… because I know none of these simple skanks out here can compete with me on my worst day. Why don't you come past my job to see me?"

"Ok I'm on the way… but you know what I like nothing more and nothing less."

I walk off the elevator and Timmy asks if I liked my surprise. Before you knew it, I had reached across the counter to snatched Timmy ass up.

"Let me tell you something….don't you ever in your motherfucking life let a stranger into my domain! Are you fucking crazy! You going to make me kill you doing some dumb shit like that. I don't know that hooker! Yeah we fucking but that's it!"

Timmy starts bitching up immediately. He's never seen me pissed off like this before.

"I'm sorry… I didn't think you were going to trip since ya'll was getting real cozy. I assumed it was cool. She said you knew! I know I fucked up. It will never happen again."

I apologize to Timmy for going that hard on him and threatening his life. I know he's trying to fit in. He's trying to do everything he can to prove he is down with the black folks.

"Timmy man, it's been a long crazy day with too much shit going on but there was no reason for me to lash out at you like that. But, don't ever, never ever do nothing like that in the future."

"Cool you got it! That dumb ass move won't ever cross my mind again."

I walk out front and flag a cab down. I tell the driver my destination. While riding I decide to make an appointment with my doctor. The receptionist asks if it's an emergency.

"Yes, something doesn't feel right with me and I need to come in soon as possible."

I tell her thanks before hanging up. Then I instruct the driver to pull over at the next stop light so I can grab something. The driver follows directions. I move fast. I hop out and within two minutes I'm back in the cab. We proceed to my destination. I pay the driver and rush to the doctor's office. I know this problem needs to be taken care of quickly. As soon as I get in, I have a seat and look around. The office isn't crowded, so that's a good thing. I walk to the front desk to sign in. The young lady asks for my information instructs me to take a seat until the doctor is ready. I take a seat, and then begin to read the magazines on the coffee table. It seems as if every magazine has something about having a baby. I quickly put each and every one of them down. I'm feeling a little tired and drained so I pull out a 5hr energy drink and throw it down my throat. I hope it hurries up and kicks in. When I glanced down at my phone I noticed three missed calls and an urgent text message from Nikki. I replied back to her. Before I could get my finger off of the send button, she responded fast as ever. From the tone of her text, you can tell that if we were talking she would be screaming. The message read:

"Who is that bitch answering your house phone? Talking about she is your baby mother and your funky ass wife to be? I pray to god that this is a joke because I don't have time for this bull shit again! I told you to stop playing with my emotions! You will die this time! I don't give a fuck if the Pope is right there, you will still be a dead man!"

"Oh hell naw! That's my stalking ass neighbor! She tricked trick Timmy into believing that we are in a relationship then he gave her a key to my shit!"

"Something ain't right! It doesn't smell good at all... fuck that, this shit stinks! But, I pray for your sake you telling me the truth."

"Boo... I promise you that I'm telling the truth and nothing but the truth; so help me god!" My scared ass replies.

"Oh nigga... you ain't in court yet but if you're lying, you will be found guilty in Nikki's court of law."

I sat there stuck in a daze wondering what the hell I'm going to do with Toya silly ass. Then I start thinking about what my mother told me previously about playing women. The receptionist calls my name to come in the back to see the doctor. She told me to put on one of those gowns, lay down on the hospital bed, and the doctor would be in shortly to see me. I follow the directions. Then Dr. Thomas comes in and greets me.

"So what brings you in today?"

"My penis won't go down for some reason and my testicals hurt. They feel like they are the size of oranges."

Doctor Thomas checks my blood pressure. Then she does an ear exam. You know the normal physical.

"I can fix your problem. It's plain to see what medicine to prescribe for you. I prescribe 1 dose of head followed by two doses of ass."

Dr. Thomas' jacket hits the floor, the exam room lights go off, next thing I know my man is in Dr. Thomas mouth. The stethoscope is on my testicals. After making my toes curl, Dr. Thomas hikes up her skirt and bends over the bed. I get to pounding to the point that Doc head hits the weight scale. I scoop her up and Ving Rhames her all the way to the counter. I put my thermometer in Doc so deep that I had to put some gauze bandages over Doc mouth, so the other patients won't hear. I stroke Doc with about 10 more hard strokes. She begins jerking like she was hit with a taser gun. I kissed Dr. Thomas.

"Call me later Meka baby... this appointment was the greatest!"

"Take two aspirin and call me in the morning."

She then gives me a kiss. I walk out the building attempting to flag down another taxi. This time I'm heading to the office. Mrs. Anderson and I are going to go over some pics from the "Private I" she hired to follow her husband around. It took a while but I finally stopped a cab. Soon as my ass hits the seat I get a call from Toya.

"You better tell your lil tricks to stop calling this damn house."

"Hooker why are you still in my house? Please tell me that is not the case! If so you must be stuck on stupid or something. Whatever it may be... get the hell out my spot hooker!" I flick off and yelled at her.

Toya in a sneaky but humble voice repeats me.

"Hooker? Oh yeah, I got your hooker! Know this brother man, you done fucked up! Your life will be destroyed day by day for fucking with me!"

"By you and what damn army! Yeah whatever! You heard what the fuck I said!"

I pull up to the front door of my office building. I shake my head in disgust. What did I get myself into? This feels like one crazy ass nightmare that I can't seem to wake up from. I start walking up the stairs to my office. When I get there I head straight into the conference room. I get detoured and stop in the bathroom to look in the mirror. I tell myself to pull it together. Never let a chick stress you out! I finally pull my shit together and go in the conference room to begin my meeting with Mrs. Anderson.

"Hello Felix... have you seen that dumb ass sister of mines or did you cut her off already? Knowing her... you probably did! She can't do shit right. It's carved in stone that she will spoil a wet dream."

I still have feelings for Rhonda so the things that she is saying are making me mad but I'm trying to keep cool.

"No I haven't talked to her... but I'm pretty sure she is in class right now or just getting out. But enough about her let's start our meeting." I said regaining control of the flow.

Mrs. Anderson looks at me with a serious beady eye look then mumbles.

"She got you too! You damn fool!"

I brush it off then and talk a little more. Mrs. Anderson slides over a manila folder for me to open. Inside the folder are different pictures of her husband on dates, shopping sprees, going into different hotels, basically balling out of control. Something in the photo's stood out. I began to look closely at the pictures. You couldn't see the young lady's face because of the angle or the hoody she had on. While looking hard at the clothes the girl was wearing I noticed something very familiar.

I grabbed a magnifying glass and looked at her jewelry while peeping her shades. It just hit me that the female in the pictures is Rhonda! He's creeping with her little sister. I remember buying her that shit when we went shopping. I always aim for one of a kind pieces like the jewelry and them sun shades. The woman is the exact same height and weight size. Why can't Mrs. Anderson see this? I drop the pictures and excuse myself from the room to gather my composure and get my thoughts together. A couple minutes go by and I return.

"Are you ok? Is something wrong?"

I'm now convinced that she has no idea that the mystery woman is her sister.

"Everything is good. I was just feeling a little nauseous."

Chapter 13

In the back of my mind I was thinking about how Rhonda wasn't really going to class all those times, she was going to meet that nigga. I find an excuse to wrap up the meeting. I've seen enough. This is some frustrating shit! I allowed myself to get played, when I do all the playing.

"I can completely focus on this case now; it's personal," I assure Mrs. Anderson.

"Why the sudden change? Why do you feel it's personal?"

"I don't like the way this guy is going about things so it's personal now."

After we exit the conference room I tell my secretary to tell everyone that I'm out of the country handling business. If they really need me they can just leave a message. In an attempt to regain my sanity, I decide to call Rick. Its football season and I haven't seen my right hand man in a minute. Just as that thought ran through my mind, my text message goes off. Its Rick telling me to meet him at MaryGold's to watch the games. He says that he has something to talk to me about. I reply back:

"That's what's up. Make sure you have the drinks ready because the kid stressed out playboy."

"You already know what it is! That's the easy part... just bring your ass here. Hurry up!"

I got a fucking headache. I walk over to the park across the street from my job and sit down on the bench. I'm just trying to regroup. I keep thinking about how I got played. It's really eating me up knowing that I got caught slipping and landed on my face. I'm the guy that never invests my feelings in women or give over my heart. I man up, reschedule my pity party, and head to meet Rick.

When I arrive at the spot it's packed with women. I'm starting to forget I'm engaged to a bad chick myself. I see Rick sitting at a table over by the bar with more bottles than a liquor store, so I make my way over.

"What's all these drinks for?"

"Didn't you say that your brain was in a frenzy? Heavy thinking requires heavy drinking. I'm just trying to help my right hand out that's all. You know I got you playboy! This that sandbox love here playboy, no fakeness."

"I thank you for that homie but what's going on? You said you had something to talk to me about."

We were interrupted by two lovely ladies that walked up to the table.

"Hey cuties... You want some company?" She asks me.

"I'm good boo... but most important, I just got engaged baby girl."

"Maybe next time fellas... but enjoy your night." She replies before walking off.

Rick smacks me in the back of the head then asked why I would say some shit like that to them sexy ass ladies. He thinks I scared them off with that foolishness.

"It's not foolishness. It's the truth cousin! I'm really about to get hitched soon."

Rick burst out laughing to the point he is choking and falling out of his chair. Then he noticed the serious look on my face. That's when he stopped laughing.

"You are crazy if you broke the code. Damn fam, you really did that shit huh," Rick asks while he shakes his head.

I hit him with the stop playing face and replied:

"Yeah, damn right I did it! But just know, it's not going to fuck up our brotherhood. Truth be told, we not getting any younger. Plus, I'm really tired of hopping from sheets to sheets. I need some stability. A person that can be my other half, you know... that other rib. You feel me pimpin?"

"I guess you right. Who's this chick you done did the "Beyonce" wit? It better not be the girl Rhonda that you just met. Fam, is she that damn good? She must know some serious tricks."

"Hell No! Fuck that bitch! She really tried to play with me, like I'm just the dumbest man to walk the earth".

"Then who is it? You don't got one of those no habla English chicks? Or, a girl that can't use your comb? If so, I know that Ma is going to kill you".

"You dumb! Hell no it's not a foreign chick or white girl. It's my baby Nikki".

"Nikki?" Rick asks with a shocked expression.

"Yeah Nikki!"

"You talking about "Love in the club" Nikki? Well she not a bad fit for you! I kinda like her for you. Awww shit, Speaking of Nikki, I know what I had to tell you now playboy".

"What is it?"

"Remember the night me and Nikki's co-worker left the club and went off to do us?"

"Yeah I remember… keep going."

"She's pregnant." Rick laughs a little and mumbles.

"You lying bruh! How is that possible! You told me all she did was give you the head, and she told Nikki all you did was ate her."

"Well, I kinda lied about that bruh. We got the kissing and rubbing, then the next thing you know, we was going for it. I didn't have no rubbers. I told her I pulled out but truth be told that shit was too good."

"Damn Shorty! You was out there playing Russian roulette with your life and got shot."

"True dat! But the wildest part is she doesn't believe in abortions. Neither one of us have kids anyway so it's not so bad."

"Especially with the life you live… you need something left behind if anything was to happen to you."

"Yeah, you right about that." Rick calmly responds.

"Congratulations playa.!"

"Thanks bro! But on a side note, remember the girl Rhonda I told you that use to spend a lot of money with me? Well she came around the way the other day to see me and told me she had a proposition for me that can earn me a lot of money."

"What is it?"

"She tells me that she wants me to kill somebody and promises me $500,000 up front and the same amount after some shit was over, but she didn't go into details."

"When did you become a contract killer or are you a damn fool?"

"When she offered me a million dollars! All the bodies I have caught for free why not get paid for doing it this time. I didn't go to some fancy law school. Nor, do I wear fancy ass suits to a six figure job. This is the only way I'm going to see a million dollars."

He jumps up mad and throws two fifty dollar bills on the table before walking off. I sit there for a second before throwing back the last shot of patron. I glance around the room looking at the various people, wondering if their life was a fucked up as mines. It seems as if everything in my world is crashing down all at once. My right hand man wants to be the eraser/hit man. Now he's a little salty at me because I don't agree with his choice. I have this crazy ass female at my place of residence that doesn't want to leave and is threatening my life. The Anderson case is deeper than money now, it's more so jealousy and envy between sisters. The sad part is I've developed feelings for Rhonda and got played in the process. Now I'm really starting to think the whole relationship was a ploy to break my concentration. If I didn't focus on the case it would get thrown on the back burner, believe it or not that's what happened. They caught me slipping; nose wide open.

My life is so complex. I have a doctor that I like a lot. I wouldn't mind seeing what could come out of it if we went to the next level. Now I'm about to get hitched and I don't know how to tell her. Topping it off, I have this sexy ass fiancé that I really only proposed to because she had her life in order. The truth is I didn't want another man to have her; but I'm scared to wife her. What am I to do with my life going into all these circles? Damn! Damn! Damn! I screamed out like Florida Evans off of "Good Times". I have no one to trust or to talk to. Things are really eating at me and I have to get myself together. I pick up the phone to call the only person that can talk me through anything. All of my trials and tribulations! I called the person that will ride with me, wrong or right.

"Hello" the person on the other end of the phone says.

"I know it's late Ma but I really need you. I'm lost in life and really don't have a clue as what to do? I don't know if I'm coming or going my brain is gone Ma."

"Baby…your brain isn't gone and you are playing tricks with your own mind. One thing I know is the lessons you were taught growing up. You are always responsible for your own actions and the decisions you make. Remember, at the end of the day… you chose to do them! You hold the key to your happiness, not 'nair one of them women you lay down with. Especially not them knuckle heads you call friends, that you have grown up with. Just take this last thing for what it's worth, you don't owe anyone anything. No one! Not even me and I gave you life! My joy will come from seeing you happy son. I love you from the bottom of my heart and that will never change! Neither has the door locks if you want to come over."

"I love you Ma. I guess you're right... only I can make myself happy at the end of the day. When you birthed me I was by myself, when I leave it will be by myself. Thanks Ma, I love you!"

Instead of going home I went back to my office to start **really** going over the documents, one paper at a time. I reviewed every expense report, every bank transaction, and every investment that was listed. Mr. Anderson was really covering up his trails well. That's when I stumbled across some child support payments. He was in arrears until he married Mrs. Anderson. That's when he began catching up because she was paying for it. Before he met her he didn't have two nickels to rub together. I got on my job with researching the name of the woman he was paying child support to. Her name is India Thomas. The name sounded really familiar but I couldn't quite figure out why. I kept asking myself why this name sounds so familiar to me. As I glanced further down the paper where I should see the child's name, it was undisclosed. Just when I thought that the riddle was cracked, a monkey wrench was thrown into my plans. But I kept pushing for more dirt. Before long I discovered that he has tripled the value of Mrs. Anderson life insurance policy, and that's strange. I peeped how every 26 days Mr. Anderson wires over $300,000 to an offshore account. What makes it even crazier is the fact that he has been doing this for the last 8 years. But, the first 4 months he was doing it every 15 days. I guess Mrs. Anderson caught wind of the money coming out of the accounts. This must've been the time he blamed the accountant or somebody that works for their company, making it seem like they were stealing the money. Mr. Anderson got smarter and figured that he would stretch it out. That's where he was wrong, Mrs. Anderson still figured it out. She's been having the money re-routed to another bank account. I bet that this dummy still thinks all the money is still overseas nice and safe.

The name India Thomas is still bothering me though. I start to think back about the past text messages that I've received. I flipped open my phone and started scrolling thru the messages. I checked each one not knowing what I was really looking for. Bingo! Here we go!

"COME AND CELEBRATE 'INDIA THOMAS' AKA MAMA THOMAS' 50th BIRTHDAY EXTRAVAGANZA AT THE 'PASH' RESTURAUNT LOUNGE BROUGHT TO YOU BY HER ONLY DAUGHTER MEKA!"

Then I start talking to myself. I'm like wow! Let me find out! Mr. Anderson is Meka's father! If this is what I think, this story is getting crazier by the minute. What's next Rhonda and Toya are sisters? Well, I guess it wouldn't be the strangest thing I heard with all this weird shit going on.

Chapter 14

I grabbed my belongings and decided to head home. I've been working so hard that I didn't even hear my phone vibrating. I've received 10 texts from Timmy. Ain't this some funny shit here, this is the same mother fucker that let that bitch in my house without calling but now he can text me. Let me see what the fuck he wants, my day can't get any worse. I call Timmy and he keeps rejecting my phone call. What the hell did he is he texting me for if he's going to reject my call? My phone vibrates again and it's a call from Timmy.

"Don't come here, police are looking for you and searching your apartment right now. Oh and guess who gave a statement, some girl that I thought was Toya but she said her name was..."

"What the fuck is going on?"

The home screen popped up on the phone. I tried to call to Timmy back but it kept going to voicemail. It's like his phone went dead or something. What the hell was going on now? This was not where I saw my life when I accepted her advances. Man, what the hell did I get myself in? I bet I'll know the next time to just keep my gun in the holster. I'm starting to see that every girl I meet isn't worth me shooting. I'm pressed for information so I call the front desk of his building thinking that Timmy would answer the phone. Instead I hear a different voice on the other end.

"Good evening Sgt. Douglas speaking… we are investigating a homicide so the staff at the front desk couldn't be here. Is there anything that I can help you with?"

I hung up that phone like the receiver was on fire and called Nikki to see if she had come home yet from Atlantic City.

"I'm not coming back home until tomorrow."

"Is there a spare key to your house somewhere?"

"What's wrong… you are scaring me acting like this!"

"It's all good. It's just a lot of crazy shit going on. I will fill you in when you come back."

"My sister is at the house with little man… so go head over there. I will call her and let them know you are on your way."

I jump in the first cab I can and give the driver Nikki's address. I laid my head back on the pleather seat hoping to get some rest. My phone starts to vibrate and Toya's name pops up.

"What bitch?"

"Was I a bitch when you beat me today? Huh nigga?"

"What the fuck you say? You have got to be trippin. I didn't touch you but if you keep fuckin' wit me… I'm gon' give you a reason to act crazy. You feel me?" I asked confused and irritated.

"Oh I feel you and so did Tonya…"

"Who the **FUCK** is Tonya? Don't play with me! I've had enough of your shit for 1 day. You a crazy ass bitch! If I ever see you again you will be dealt with!"

I hung up before she could respond. She kept calling back and I kept sending her ass to voicemail. Then she decided to text me. It was picture mail. I dread even opening it but I did. It's a picture of a sonogram. Aww hell naw!!!!!!!!! Just then the cab stopped and I realized that I was in front of Nikki's house. I paid the cab fare and slammed the door, mad at the world. Right now I could kill someone. The mere thought of this hooker claiming to be with child is too much for me. And, who the hell is Tonya? Man, I swear your boy ain't never been this confused. What am I to do? Anybody can be with child just not this dumb ass broad! I sit on Nikki's porch and hang my head in shame. My phone rings again.

"What bitch?" I say without looking at the screen.

"Damn, I'm your bitch now? You know the only time you can call me that is when we rocking, other than that watch your tone." Meka snapped.

"I'm sorry baby…I'm just frustrated. No hard feelings… but what's up Miss Lady?"

"I got some good news for you that will cheer you up."

"I hope so with this day I'm having."

"I just saved a $100.00 on my car insurance." She burst out laughing.

"Good one!" I laughed cause Lord knows I needed that.

"All jokes aside Felix… I'm pregnant boo."

The phone hangs up. I just fall to the ground, look to the clouds, and scream. *"Why me Lord, please tell me why me?"* What did I do to deserve this shit here? Man, my Mama told me when it rains it pours. It seems as if God wants in on the joke because at that moment it literally began to rain. I just sat there in the rain on stuck, wondering what else can go wrong. After a few minutes I get up, dripping wet, and ring the door bell. Nikki sister comes to the door looking just like a younger version of Nikki. I'm in a momentary daze because she doesn't have any kids so her body is on one million. She's looking good as hell!

"Are you going to stand out there in the rain or are you coming in?"

I was a little stuck for a minute. I was thinking with the wrong head again. Shit, thinking with my magic stick is what got me into all this shit now. As I walk in I speak to Nikki's sister and son. I make my way to the spare room, plop onto the bed, and put a pillow over my head to muffle my screams.

Something has to change in my life. I mean really change fast! I guess I finally feel asleep. I have 3 million things running through my mind so nightfall turned into the morning real fast. The sun beamed in on my back through the open curtains. I opened my eyes to find Nikki starring at me. She startled me so I jumped back because I don't remember her climbing in the bed. I sit up placing my head into my hands. Nikki grabbed the remote and turned on the TV. It was on Channel 4.

"So tell me, what's going on with you."

I started to tell her about Toya and what Timmy told me. A news woman interrupted some court show that was playing.

"We interrupt our regularly scheduled programming for a late breaking story. D.C. police are searching for a suspect that is believed to have some information on a brutal attack that occurred in the 1200 block of M St, NW last night. This attack left one person dead and another injured. If you know of this persons' whereabouts please contact crime solvers hotline, there's a $50,000 reward for information leading to his capture."

Just like that, I was a wanted felon. They posted a picture of me on the screen. Nikki's mouth dropped to the floor.

"Boy, who the hell did you kill? And you trying to hide out over here... knowing I got a damn kid! Nigga you are fucking unbelievable and crazy...!

Then she tells herself to calm down. She's a rider and it's me and her against the world.

"...So did you do it?"

"C'mon now you know me! Hell no! I didn't kill nobody! It's that crazy bitch that answered the phone when you called."

"Awww... brother, you all over the news. What you done did boy? You lucky you with big sis or that 50k would be mine!" Nikki's sister decided to add her two cents.

"Did you say 50k? That sounds like 25 a piece huh? Sike! I can't send my baby to jail."

The phone rings. It's my mother screaming about telling her the truth.

"Boy, you got the whole church calling me. Sister Ellis done called Sister Margaret, then she called Brother James, and he called Pastor Josh who called me. They said **my son** is wanted for murder! Who the hell did you kill boy?"

"Ma...calm down. Please tell your congregation that I didn't kill anybody! Mama, I'm going to need a lot of prayer for this one here."

"Do you have a lawyer? When are you going to the station? I'm gon' have the entire church there in full force."

"Ma I have the best lawyer in town. He went to school with me. I'm going to call him now and then I'm going to go turn myself in."

I call my good friend Cassuis Greer, whose name rings in this city for beating big murder cases.

"I already know what's going on. It's on every news channel playboy."

"So you've seen it to C? Now what am I supposed to do?"

"Tell me what happened...everything! Then I'll meet you at the precinct so that you can "check in." You'll be out on bail in no time…"

I give him a run down everything that occurred that day. I told him how Toya showed up butt naked at my house. How she moved all my furniture out and then promised to make my life miserable since I didn't want to be with her.

"… aw shit! You got some serious fatal attraction shit on your hands. Ain't nothing like a woman that's scorned. She is willing to go through hell and back, to fuck your life up."

"We got to fix this quick bruh! I mean fast!"

Cassuis said he would call me when he got back to D.C. He was in Richmond, VA but was on his way. I want to cry but I can't let Nikki see me go out like that. This shit is stressing a brother out. I know the only person that can really help me out of this situation is The Lord Jesus Christ himself! I hit my knees so fast they went into shock and I began to pray.

"Father above if you can help get me out of this trouble that I'm in, I will change my outlook on life. I will change the way I handle things. I know that I'm a grown ass man now and I have to be responsible for all my actions. I know I can't keep running around like I'm that 25 year old gigolo I used to be. I know I have to begin planning for the next generations to come. It's no more thinking for self, I understand. So Father, if you can help a young man that has been lost along the way, I would be more than thankful. Amen"

I head down to the precinct to meet Cassuis thinking this is going to be a in and out procedure, boy was I was sadly mistaken. The plan was to request a bond. The judge had other plans. She threw a monkey wrench into my plans. Man, them peoples put the handcuffs on me and stepped me behind the metal door. They walked me to the holding cell and opened the bars like they were doors to a 5 star hotel. I walked over and sat on the bench/ bed. It had a thin ass mattress. I tried to occupy my mind by reading the names written on the walls. That shit worked for about five minutes. As I sit here, my life is flashing before my eyes. I begin to reflect on these last couple of years. I spent a lot of time focusing on the last couple of months. I guess I'm trying to weigh certain shit. How can I justify losing the rest of my life over a female? I was blessed to be a lawyer but I wasn't taking my job serious enough. I was so wrapped up into getting as much pussy as possible, I wasn't even focused on the biggest case of my life. It was going to make me the youngest partner of the firm ever! I can't believe I was throwing that all away for some ego boost. At the end of the day that's all it was, something to make me feel like the man. I now realize that in life we are greedy when it comes to relationships, we bite off more than we can chew. Women get tired of the same men since the whole independent movement started. We as men know that it's 33 women to 1 man in D.C., but, knowing that doesn't mean we're supposed to have all 33.

It's jive sad to know I waited until something tragic happened before I became ready to change shit. Days turned into weeks. I haven't eaten in I don't know when. I'm weak and my life is passing me by. I'm miserable at this point. Finally, Cassuis came to visit with the best news I've ever wanted to hear.

"The building surveillance along with a lot of other evidence proves your innocence. But, the most important thing is that in a few hours, you'll be a free man. "

Tears of joy dropped from my eyes knowing my prayers have been answered. I hit my knees and said, Thank you Jesus! Thank you!" I was not only thankful to be free, I was thankful to be in jail because if I'd seen Toya, I would've killed her.

"Do you know a Toya or a Tonya? She's mentally disturbed. She has multiple personalities. She likes to assume the role of her dead sister. She's are armed and dangerous. If you see her, stay away. She's killed and has no problem killing again." Cassuis warned.

As soon as the wind hit my face I called Nikki to tell her we got a wedding to plan over the next couple of weeks.

"Are you ready?"

"Hell yeah… you know I am… but why the sudden rush?"

"I had a chance to think about the things. Marrying you is number 1 and the second thing is to win the case for Mrs. Anderson."

As soon as I say that my line beeps. I click over:

"Hello…

There is no response, so I say it again

"…Hello? Who is this?"

"It's Rick… I really need your help son! This is life or death."

"Where are you at playboy?"

Rick's talking in codes like he always does.

"I'm a block over from candy man post up spot."

"Stay there… I will be there in a second."

I'm fresh out the joint on the way to help my man. I have no idea what I'm walking into but that's my man so I'm going. I make it over to where Rick is in 15 minutes flat. I call for him to come outside. When Rick opens the door he is covered in blood. I hurry up and push him back inside. After making sure the blood wasn't his, I calmed down.

"You did it… didn't you? Don't say nothing because I know you tried that dumb shit!"

"Yeah… I did it. To me it felt like easy money but shit went wrong!" Rick says

"What happened? Why you think it went wrong?" I ask

Rick tells me the story the way it went down from the beginning to the end.

"The chick that hired me called earlier. She said that her and some dude would be at the mall. They would be parked in the parking garage and I was supposed to meet them there. I get to the garage, and I lay low 3 cars down from where they parked at. I see them walk out so I creep up behind them, then fake like I was about to rob them. First, I snatch his bags. Then I grab her purse... she's jive feisty so she bucks back. That's when I let loose. I shot her like 3 times and rolled out. I know I hit her from point blank range. Now I'm thinking the job was finished until I received a text message saying that she's still alive. They say I fucked up and now the finger is pointing to her husband. He's threatens to point the finger my way on some hot sucker shit, so I snatch up his prize possession. Through that ass in the trunk of my car and now I'm holding it for leverage."

"What is it? What have you taken from this dude that he will feel that strong about that he won't tell on you?"

"I can show you better than I can tell you! Follow me."

I go with Rick. As soon as we enter I start looking around. I don't see anything. I follow Rick down a long hallway. The building stinks. It smells like piss, ass, and bad breath. Rats are bungee jumping from the steps. The walls are covered with holes and blood. It's like something out of a horror movie. He takes the padlock off of the door and pushes it open. It's a woman. Her head is hung down. He snatches her by the back of her head, making her face visible to me. I can't believe my eyes. He snatches the duct tape from her mouth. She screams in pain.

"Surprise! Tada! Look at this shit here playboy!"

"Felix….help me," Rhonda begs.

I rush over to untie her from the chair. I know Rick's not going to shoot me, so I'm not worried.

"Yo wait a minute…Felix, you know this dope fiend ass bitch?"

"This is Rhonda that I have been dating. The one I took to Atlantic City that I told you I was falling for."

Chapter 15

"Naw man! Say it ain't so! You wasn't really falling for this dick sucking slut! No wonder she disappeared, but she couldn't stay away to long. Once a fiend always a fiend! This bitch thinks I'm gonna take the fall for her and that square ass bama she fucking, she's wrong. I can't believe you fell for this bitch!" Rick proclaims as he smacks her with the gun handle.

"C'mon man, let her go. I'll help you get out of this."

"Naw man! I can't do that! This fiend right here is my ticket out of this shit."

"C'mon man she's bleeding like a hog! Let her go!"

"Let me find out my nigga got a heart for a clucker! Man you soft for this trick ass drug addict?"

"I can't let you hurt her Rick! When I met her and fell for the young lady she was clean. If you really want to know, yeah I still got feelings for her, fiend or not."

"You are becoming a real sucker for love you know that? Like I said, this my ticket."

"She's not your ticket, I'm your ticket nigga! Listen to what I'm telling you! Slow down…I'm the lady you shot lawyer. I'm handling her case! Believe me, that nigga is not getting away scott free! Hell no! You got to trust me! This that sandbox shit you were talking about the other day. I got you fam! You don't have to worry about shit! Look at me man, this is your brother you talking to."

"Man…I feel what you are saying but I got to kill this bitch! This bitch whole intentions was to set me up from the beginning. She thought her and that nigga was gon' sit back and point the finger at me. I ain't going out like that. This bitch is going to die today. And, I want the rest of my mother fucking money…you hear me bitch? You better hope your man brings my money." He screams while smacking her again with the gun.

"C'mon man… you can't shoot her! It's not worth it! Listen to me! I'm with you! I got your back!"

"Why you trying to be Captain Save-A-Fiend? You shedding tears for this modern day Pooky? I'm not taking the fall for this bitch!"

Rick cocks his gun. Rhonda screams but it's pointless. Nobody can hear her since we are in abandoned buildings. Rick kicks her in the mouth with his Timbs as he yells for her to shut the fuck up. He spreads his legs into his killer stance and point the gun at her head. Before he could squeeze the trigger, I rushed him from behind and did a superman dive onto him. The gun released several shots. My head slammed against the floor. The room is pitch black. A scream filled the room that made my skin crawl. Instantly the room smelled like gun powder and death. I check myself frantically to make sure that I'm not hit. I snatch the board from the window so I can see. With the light, I can see that I'm covered in blood. I check myself again to see if I've been shot. As I wipe the blood from my face I'm still having a hard time focusing. I see a blurry image of a body lying in a puddle of blood. I hurry over to find Rick laying on the floor gasping for air. The gunshot wound is to his upper body and blood is running out like water. I take off my shirt trying to apply pressure and slow down the bleeding. Rick is mouthing something to me. He starts to cough up blood and his eyes begin to roll back into his head. I really start panicking. This is my best friend, my cousin, my blood…he can't die like this.

"Call 911…hold on Rick! Hold on!" I screamed at Rhonda.

Rhonda is freaking out, not knowing what to do. She's crying and shaking. Blood is draining from her open skull.

"You got to untie me."

I don't want to let up on the pressure but I have to free her to make the call. I free her hands and toss my cell to her. I rush back to Rick's side.

"I swear if my brother dies, that's your ass bitch! You better hope they get here in time."

I start telling Rick to calm down everything is going to be ok. Rick tries to talk but it's so much blood on his tongue, he's gagging. His body begins to seize and then I watched helplessly as he took his last breath. I feel like I've been stabbed in the heart. My grief quickly turned to anger. Rhonda had freed herself from the chair and was standing over Rick and I. I grabbed for Rhonda but she moved away. She bawled up into a fetal position and slid down the wall onto the floor crying.

"Here bitch! Is this what you wanted? Did your plans work? Because of some fake ass scheme you and that fagot ass nigga came up with… my right hand man is dead!

I grab the gun from Rick's lifeless hand and turned to Rhonda. I pointed the gun at her.

"… you're next!" I declare.

"No please! No! I'm sorry! I never thought it was going to end like this. We just wanted to be happy! Please don't kill me!"

"Shut the fuck up! Was you crying when you set my man up? Was you crying when you played me? Huh? Either way, my man's life was going to be fucked up because you were going to point the finger at him. Somebody got to pay for this situation right here! And… since you here right now, it's time for you to cash in."

I go to shoot her but my arm is shaking. I still have feelings for her even though she just ran my ass in a circle. I'm not a killer. Rhonda can sense that I'm not going to shoot her.

"Boo… we can work this out! I was about to cut him off to make way for us! Please don't give up on us! I love you!"

She walks towards me trying to rub my arm in a sneaky manor. The shit was almost working, until I saw Rick on the floor and snapped out of it.

"You got me fucked Shorty! Yeah you're good… but not that damn good! I let your ass work me once but not again."

I grabbed her by the throat, placing the gun nozzle onto the tip of her nose. Just as I was about to blow her fucking head off, the police come charging into the building! I forgot that Rhonda called them. They used the phones' GPS signal to track us down.

"Freeze! Drop the weapon or we will shoot!"

I toss the gun in front of the officer's foot carefully. I wanted him to know I was not a threat. They rushed me throwing me onto the dirty floor and then they cuffed me.

"You better tell them what happened and make it light on yourself, Miss Lady. Tell them how you got my best friend killed. Tell them how you tried to kill your sister. The truth is going to come out. You better make it light on yourself."

She paused for a second as if she was going to let the police take me into custody.

"Officer, leave him. He didn't do anything. I'm the one responsible for this. If it wasn't for my actions, nobody would have died. I'm ready to deal with whatever I have to face."

"We'll take you both and work it out at the station."

The police locked Rhonda up but still took me in for questioning. I mean I did have a gun to her head when they walked in. After spending hours at the precinct they let me go. Rhonda's lawyer worked something out for her in exchange for setting up Mr. Anderson. She had to try to get him to confess to conspiracy to commit murder on his wife. While all of this was going on, my soon to be wife is pissed. She has been calling me all day but, because of all this shit that has been happening today, I never

143

answered. She's hot as fish grease, I just know it. I flipped the phone open and called.

"What nigga? You been ducking me all damn day! I sure hope that trick was worth it!"

"It wasn't no trick…Rick is dead!"

"Oh my God! Baby…I'm so sorry."

"Wait it's more to it."

"Never mind…it doesn't matter. I don't want to mess your day up more than it already is!"

"It can't get no worst then this boo! So what were you trying to tell me?"

"I went to the doctor today…

I broke out grinning. I think I know what she's about to say. I pressed my ear close to the phone.

"… they told me that I have colorectal cancer. Remember the stomach aches I was complaining about. Well they say that is spreading fast."

"How long?"

"There's no definite way to tell it could be 4 months or 4 years. I can beat it with the proper treatment. So if you don't want to marry me now... I fully understand..."

It's total silence. You can hear a pin drop.

"...Felix...baby...did you hear me?"

I don't know what happened after that. I think I passed out. I came to, on the ground with the phone in my hand. What the hell is going on? I get myself together and call Nikki back.

"Baby, I'm sorry. I think I fainted. You caught me off guard with that news. I thought you were going to tell me we created a new life, I wasn't expecting to hear your dying."

"Well I'm sorry if my news wasn't to your liking. I wasn't jumping for joy when I heard it either. I will just go off and die alone."

"That's the last thing I want you to do boo! Stop talking like that! You rode with me through all this dumb shit and I'm going to ride with you till the wheels fall off! When I asked you to be my wife, I meant it. The lifestyle that I got so comfortable with nearly killed me. I almost fucked my life up to the point of no return. Baby, remember that you are all ever I want! We're going to beat this cancer shit together!"

Out the corner of my eye, I see that crazy ass chick Toya, Tonya or whatever the fuck her name is. She's standing there in a got damn wedding dress holding flowers like she is about to walk down the aisle. I blink my eyes really fast, trying to focus. This can't be real. When I open my eyes and look again, there she is. I tell Nikki that I will call her back. My voice cracked like I'd seen a ghost. I took off running across the street full speed, yelling out "B*itch I'm going to kill you!"*

Chapter 16

When I get to the center of the road, I stopped to let the Metrobus past. It's moving too fast to chance it. By the time the bus passes, I look again to see that this loony tune has disappeared. I don't know where she has vanished to. This shit got me feeling like The Ghost Whisperer or something. I got so caught up that I forgot I was standing in the middle of the road. In efforts to dodge one car and I ran smack into a Ford F-150 pickup.

Everything goes blank. When I regain consciousness I'm in a helicopter being flown to the hospital. I have all of this stuff hooked to me. My mind is semi-alert but my body is not responding to what I'm saying.

I drifted off into thought. My life flashed before my eyes in snapshots. I remember back to the day when my mother pushed me out the womb. I see a flash of my first fist fight I had with my best friend Rick when we were about 7 years old. I got a flash of the day I wrote the "will you go with me" letter. You know the one, circle yes or no. I saw my first time kissing Rachel Brooks. She was my first grade love. We kissed behind the sliding board after lunch time at recess. A bright light covered me. I can hear the angels sing a soulful melody in my head. A smile crosses my face. Am I dead? I don't know how long I've been here. I see flashes of people like my mom and Nikki. I can hear people talking about pulling a plug. I just can't tell if it's a dream or if they're really here with me. I suddenly hear a familiar voice.

"No one and I mean **no one**... will every love you like I do."

I feel a warm kiss against my forehead. My body jumps as if I've been electrocuted and my eyes pop open. I scared the shit of the person standing beside me because they jumped and almost knocked over the IV stands and heart monitor. This is a cruel ass joke. All that I've been through and the first person I see when I open my eyes is Toya or Tonya. This bitch is dressed like a nurse, smock and all.

"What are you doing to me?" I mustered the strength to ask as I tried to raise up.

"I told you that you fucked with the wrong one! See Toya's compassionate ass took it light on you... but I'm going to finish it!"

I'm trying to talk but can't quite get myself together. I start kicking the bed while frantically looking for the call bell. I don't have the strength to fight her off. She's holding a syringe in her hand. I'm kicking at her, reaching for the bell, and praying that someone comes in the room; then she places her finger over my mouth.

"Shhhhh…calm down. I'm going to take good care of you."

She bends over and gives me a kiss. I heard Nikki's voice coming down the hall and threw the bed pan as far as I could. Toya/ Tonya retreated and rolled out before having a chance to use the syringe. She managed to get out of the room before Nikki entered. I look towards the door to see who was with Nikki and it's my mother. As soon as they see me alert and moving, they begin to holler.

"God is good! Thank you Father, thank you! Thank you for delivering my baby from that coma. I knew you were merciful! Hallelujah" my mother screamed from her knees.

Nikki's tears raced down their cheeks as she stared at me in disbelief. Apparently, I have been in a coma for two weeks. I'm lying here with a tear in my eye and an angry face! I'm mad that the reason I'm here, half dead, was just in the room with me. If they hadn't arrived I would be dead for sure. My mother noticed how agitated I look.

"Baby how are you feeling?'

I struggled to relay my message but couldn't get the words together.

"Toya..." I whispered, "she was here..."

"What you say baby?"

"Nurse...Toya"

"What the hell did that nurse do to you while she was just in here?"

She pressed the button to call down for a doctor or someone who could help me. A nurse responded.

"What was the nurses' name that was just in with my son?"

"The last person to come in here was me but that was a hour and a half ago, I'm your son's nurse. I don't have a clue as to who that was."

"Tonya." I mumble.

"What did you say son?"

"Toya...here...tried to kill me," I say with a little more strength.

"I swear to God I'm going to beat that bitch ass when I catch her! She is doing too damn much!" Nikki screams.

"Get some rest son. We're not going to leave your side until you are out of here. Let that bitch come back while I'm here. I got something for that ass!"

"Baby…your mother and I went to Ricks funeral. We sent your condolences', prayers, and blessings to the family. We also ordered a nice flower display on your behalf."

Tears began pouring from my eyes like sweat from a marathon runner. It just donned on me that this shit is not a bad dream, it really happened. Rick is dead! I forgot that my best friend is no longer here with me. This bitch has robbed me of everything. My best friend is dead, the Anderson case is all fucked up, and this psycho bitch is trying to erase me. My life is in shambles. I don't even know where it went wrong.

Days turn into weeks, and weeks turn into months. The rehabilitation process is grueling. I have to learn how to do everything over. Walk, talk, eat, everything! Nikki has been taking care of things for me. She's shown that she is the definition of a down as chick! She handled the sale of my condo, had my numbers changed, and has been a great help to my mom. Every since that shit with Tonya/Toya stalking me and shit, I had to switch everything up. I sit in the chair closest to the window, I refuse to keep laying in that damn bed. I got to get out of here.

"There's someone here to see you?" said Nikki.

"When I grow up I want to be like you, partner!" Stan announces with a big smile.

"I'm a partner now? You serious?"

"Yes you sure are son! Congratulations! We can't wait to have you back. The team misses you."

"What happened with Mrs. Anderson case?"

"Well…Mr. Anderson was at the hospital bedside of Mrs. Anderson. She's been attacked and shot by an unknown assailant. But the kicker is, he sat beside her crying and putting on a hell of a show, like he was so concerned. He swore at the top of his lungs that he would find out who was responsible. Then Mrs. Andersons' younger sister shows up to visit her. She brings her some flowers, balloons, you know the usual. It was about 4 or 5 people in the room when she arrives. Anyway, Mr. Anderson tells Rhonda he needs to talk to her out in the hallway for a second. At the time no one thinks anything of it because everyone knows Mr. Anderson doesn't like to have conversations around people. Everyone just thought it was personal family business. They begin to walk away from the room so no one can hear the conversation."

Stan placed a mini recorder on the bed and pressed play.

"I don't feel right and this shit is starting to eat away at me. I didn't care at first but at the end of the day, she's my big sister. I still love her, no matter how much drama she puts me through. We are blood!"

"She was blood when you were fucking me, wasn't she? Fuck her! You know damn well, we did the right thing. She was going to bleed me dry. I made that money, not her. Shit, I would've paid a lot more, and hired someone who would've finished the mission."

"What we did was wrong and fucked up! If it weren't for her, there would be no you. You didn't have a dime when she met you! She upgraded your life! What gives you the right to try to take hers?"

"Ha...ha...ha...just know my money grows on trees. Don't bite the hand that feeds you! Now if you want to be stupid enough to go against me, after I finish with her you can follow. Better yet, I will pay double for ya'll to leave together like your parents did. Don't play with me! Keep your mouth shut!"

Rhonda doesn't say anything.

"...I knew you would see it my way." Mr. Anderson proclaims.

Stan cuts off the tape recorder. So they walk back to the room where Mrs. Anderson was. Her guests were undercover police officers. They were waiting for Mr. Anderson to confess. They locked him up for conspiracy to commit murder on his wife. As they were taking him away, he looked at Rhonda, who opened up her suit jacket and revealed the wire she was wearing. She smiled at him and he tried to break free from the police. He went off, calling her every bitch in the book. He managed to spit in her face. It was something straight out of a movie Stan explained.

"Are you serious?"

"Oh no, it gets better. Rhonda wiped the spit from her face, then hauls off and slaps the shit out of Mr. Anderson. Then she screams that he is a no good, two faced, little dick having ass nigga, that is just good for eating coochie. And, oh Yeah don't drop the soap faggot..."

We all crack up laughing. I can't believe it ended like that. I'm glad they got that mother fucker! He was a poor excuse for a man.

"...His divorce case got dropped and all the money was awarded to Mrs. Anderson. All $967 million dollars! She made a big contribution to you and the firm."

"God is good! The rain is just a step before the sun shines! I'm glad everything worked out with that case."

"All's well that ends well!"

Our conversation was interrupted when the Doctor came in. If I can pass my physical in the morning, I'm clear to go home. I'm excited but nervous as hell. My left leg keeps going numb from time to time. I'm going to put it in God's hands. The doctor excuses himself and says that he will see me later today.

"Well son...we will see you when you get back to work. Be prepared to work, partner! The office hasn't been the same without you and that constantly ringing phone of yours."

"I can't wait! I will be back better than ever."

Chapter 17

The day passes along slowly. My mother invited some members of her church up to the hospital for a minute to pray over me. I tried not to think too much about the physical but knowing it determines if I'm ready to be released gives it priority in my brain. After the prayer, my mothers' prayer warriors exit the room. Now I'm alone with my mother and Nikki.

"Nikki...I'm so happy that you're going to be a part of my family. You'll fit in just fine with the rest of the fools," Mom laughs.

Then she kisses me on the cheek then tells me that I have good thing with Nikki. She followed with the threat that I better not screw up.

"I'm not going to mess up, I promise!"

"Ok, I'm going to leave you two love birds alone. Momma is going home so I can rest this old body of mines. You get some rest, you have a long day ahead of you tomorrow."

"I will see you in the morning. Love ya, Ma!"

I continue my conversation with Nikki, but in the back of my mind I keep wondering what Meka is up to? Most of all, is she still lugging my baby around? And, if so, how do I tell my future wife that Meka is having my first child? I tried to fight it but they came gushing down my face once the reality set in. Thoughts of Rick crowded my mind. He's no longer here to talk my problems out with and his death is my fault. I really broke down.

"I don't know what you are thinking but everything will be good! Somehow…some way, we're going to make it. God has a plan for us all."

Night time falls upon me but I can't sleep. I can't stop thinking that Tonya's crazy ass is going to pop in and try to kill me in my sleep. I'm so nervous about the physical in the morning as well. I've had my share of curve balls that were thrown at me these past months. The sun peeps in threw the window letting me know, that I must've finally drifted off. It's judgment time! I feel like I just went to sleep. As my eyes come into focus, I see the first Doctor walk in. Then after about 15 to 20 minutes go by, three more doctors come in.

"Okay young man…let's see how you're doing."

"I sure am ready to get out of here Doc."

The physical begins as they do numerous drills. First they try the walk alone task without a cane, crutch, or helping hand. I stand up to take some steps and my left leg goes numb. I fall to one knee knowing that I can't hold my balance. The doctors begin scribbling notes on my chart. I refuse to quit so I try again. God blesses me with momentary strength. I stand and then begin to move my legs one step at a time. I feel like a toddler taking their first steps. I get excited and immediately start praying, knowing that I'm ready for the world again. The Doctor's decide to release me with a few restrictions. I have to walk with a cane. I also have to get glasses because I've lost 45% of vision in my left eye. I guess you can say that I'm legally blind.

My mother and Nikki grab my bags as we prepare to leave. I feel funny riding in this wheelchair. We make it to the open car door. As I prepare to transfer from the wheelchair into the car, a black SUV speeds by. The screeching of the tires broke my concentration and I fell onto the ground. Gun shots rang out. People were running everywhere and screaming. One of the bullets hit Nikki. Her car was riddled with bullet holes. As the vehicle sped off I can hear a female screaming, you will die bitch! I recognize the voice off the break. I know for a fact it was "Toya or Tonya" crazy ass trying to kill me. The doctors rush to Nikki's aide and rush her to E.R. Had I been on the other side of the car, it would've been me. That crazy bitch almost shot my mother!

"This bitch has pushed my last button. She must die! This hooker shot at my mother and she hit my fiancé… fuck that! It's on! Since the law can't catch her ass… I bet I will."

How do we go from celebrating my release to my future wife shot up in E.R.? My life is fucked up. It changes from bad to worse in a matter of minutes. Who would have ever thought that my past would come back to haunt me like this? I feel if they would have let me die, maybe everybody else's life would be peaceful. I start kirking off! I feel like they are not working as fast as they can to help Nikki. I don't know what I'll do if something happens to her.

"Calm down son. The lord has this one. He hasn't let you down yet."

"Why me Lord… why me? I'm a great dude."

"What makes you think you don't have to go through anything when that man above has shed a lot of blood? What makes you think you are not going to have to shed some blood?"

"You're right Ma."

A flurry of white coats and hospital outfits came rushing by. They were running into the room where Nikki was being worked on. I start to panic as I get closer to the room. The nurse is trying to stop me from entering but I can hear the machine flat line. I watch helplessly through the glass as they yell for the defibrillator to bring her back. He yells clear and my heart stops. I can't contain my emotions. I start banging on the glass.

"Please God don't let her die! Please take me instead! Let her live her life! It's all my fault...punish me not her".

The machine begins to beep and my eyes are glued to the wavy lines. The surgeon said that they successfully removed the bullet. She's lost a lot of blood but she's a fighter. They said that the bullet was less than 1 inch away from her heart. If she would've sneezed, she would've died. They push her into the recovery room where she's heavily sedated. She's definitely in la la land.

"That was a close one! If it had been a finger nail length longer over to the right it would have penetrated her heart. The good thing is an angel was over her today so that's all that matters. You can go in there to see her now."

"Thank you Doctor."

My mother pushed my wheelchair into the recovery room where she slept. She placed me alongside Nikki's hospital bed.

"Take your time son. I'm going to go meet her sister downstairs."

"Thanks Ma."

I sat there for a second, lost. I didn't know what to say or do. Everything happened so fast. I am destroying everything I love. I gently rubbed her hair. She's so beautiful and because of me she's unconscious. Tears began to roll down my face. I took her hand and began to apologize for everything that has been happening. I didn't mean for none of this shit to take place.

"I know that you are out of it right now… but just know that I love you to the fullest! Yep I said it, I Felix Williams am in love with you Nikki."

Rashida, Nikki's sister comes barreling through the door with a face full of tears.

"Felix, look what did you do to my sister?"

"Calm down sis… everything is going to be ok! I'm going through it… just like you are! Maybe even worst! She's the only person I could have considered asking for her hand in marriage. I don't know what I would do without her and lil' man… by the way, where is my little man?"

"He's in the waiting room with his father. Your mom met us downstairs. You kinda favor her a little bit."

"Why are they in the waiting room instead of being in here with Nikki?"

"They said that lil' man is too young but he can see her when she relocates to her room. Chris didn't want to be disrespectful by walking right in here...you know since ya'll getting married and everything."

"I'm a man! I understand he cares for her too. They have a child together. I won't feel any disrespect. It's no secret that he was in her life first and if he needs me to step I will do so, that's nothing."

She goes to tell Chris what I said. As he walks in I begin to roll my wheelchair out the way and give him a few ticks of privacy. I know he got to be feeling some kind of way about this shit. I know I still can't believe what has happened.

"You don't have to leave Champ! What I have to say is more so for you. I always said when I met you I would thank you for being in my son's life while I was locked up. It's not too many niggas that take another man's kid in like they are theirs. I respect that a lot. You was never on no bama shit when I called from the pen. You showed mad respect! Not on no sucker shit but on some grown man shit! That's rare out here these days."

"Man, I just tried to do what I would want somebody to do for me if the tables were turned. I knew that your son stayed there, so some lines of communication got to be open. At the end of the day, a lion recognizes another lion, so that's what it is."

"True dat! You and Nik have my blessings. You have a good girl on your side. Hey, who knows… maybe me and my little shorty, Meka might follow suit. We might take a page from your book and do thc marriage thang."

Chapter 18

I had to pause for a second. I then shook my head naw. He can't be talking 'bout my Meka. I extend my hand to Chris to give him a hand shake. He gives me some dap, kisses Nikki on the forehead, and starts to leave the room.

"Now you know we have to find a way to break the rules. I'm 'bout to sneak little man in here right quick, so he can see his mother and give her a kiss."

"You know I don't care nothing 'bout no rules," Chris responds.

He returns with lil man who is holding a handful of balloons for his mother. He's scared and sad. He begins to cry.

"What's up lil man… how you been?"

"Why are you in a wheelchair and what's wrong with mommy?"

"The devil was trying to get me and your mother… but God protected us!"

"So is God like Batman and Superman?"

"God is 100 times better than them other guys."

Little Chris climbs slowly up onto the bed and gives his mother a kiss. He whispers, "*I love you mommy*" in her ear before climbing down. He gives me a hug and then begins to leave with his father.

"Can you tell my mom's to come back here? I want her to pray for Nikki."

"Sure...no problem," Chris replies.

Chris and lil' man returned in about 3 minutes with my mother. We join hands and my Mom says a prayer for Nikki.

"Do you want me to stay up here with you?"

"No thanks...go ahead and go home. Rest yourself. This has been a day that won't ever be forgotten! I'm ok. I'm going to stay with Nikki!"

I spend most of the night just praying to get the devilish thoughts out of my head. I can't stop thinking about killing Toya/ Tonya. I grabbed the remote and turned the TV on. The 11:00 news has just begun. I watched the report recorded live from the hospital entrance. It seems like a dream. I was there but I swear this shit doesn't seem real. Then a sketch of Tonya/Toya popped up. I turned the sound up.

"If you see this woman...do not approach her. She suffers from DID, Dissociative Identity Disorder, or multiple personalities. The suspect may be using the name Toya or Tonya. She is wanted in connection with several homicides and is armed and dangerous!"

I asked myself how the hell did I fall for that crazy ass chick? The great acrobatic stunts and bomb ass head wasn't worth all of this heartache! I should have left her ass on that elevator with her stripper case. I knew that she was trouble from the start. But, she was serving up sex like Burger King. She let me have it my way. I'm usually a good judge of character but she fooled me. I continued having flash backs about her crazy ass for a few minutes. Nikki's heart monitor goes off. The doctors rush in, she's flat lined for the second time. It's really taking its toll on me as I begin to tear up. I know that the first time was a scare and this one is the real thing. I guess it's been about thirty to forty minutes. The doctors have been working nonstop to revive her and finally they have stabilized her heart.

"You wife lost a lot of blood. She suffered some internal bleeding before the operation. The trauma is causing her to have mini seizures which causes the heart beat to stop.

She is stable right now although her body is in shock. I expect her to make a full recovery. It's going to be fine. She will be fine and she will not realize what has taken place. It's like she is having a great sleep."

"Thanks for everything you've done to help my fiancé to see another day on this earth with me."

The sun rose so fast, I know I haven't shut my eyes for more than 15 minutes or so. Sleeping in this damn wheelchair is not the business. Before I could get the sleep out of my eyes the doctors where busy running tests. They were finally ready to move her from ICU to a regular room. She's going to be in here for a couple of days, at least she can have visitors. My mother comes in shortly after the doctors with a change of clothes for me. I've been sitting in the same fit from yesterday and that's a no no! I've got to be on point at all times because you never know who you gon' meet.

The hours roll along. Me, lil' man, Rashida, and my mom's sat around talking and watching TV. As long as I am close to Nikki, I'm fine. Lil' Chris walks over to his mother's bedside. He tells her that he loves her, and really misses her so much. Then he gives her a kiss on the hand. Suddenly, Nikki's eyes open. Chris begins to yell out that she's not sleep anymore, "Mommy is up." Nikki glances around the room trying to figure out what's going on and why is she hooked up to these machines.

"Felix what's going on? Where am I? Why am I here?" Nikki asks in terror.

"Do you remember anything that happened a few days ago?"

"What do you mean a few days ago? I remember us walking you out the front door. We were getting in the car, and then I heard a vehicle slam on breaks. I thought it was a collision until I heard something that sounded like the fourth of July. Everything after that is a blur."

"Baby, it was Tonya crazy ass in that car. She pulled up and opened fire on us. You were shot in the chest. Somehow she found out that I was being released, so she tried to finish me off. I'm sorry you got caught up in this. She's gon' be dealt with, believe me. Now, don't you worry your pretty little head about this! I just want you to think about how good you're going to look in that wedding dress."

Over the next couple of days Nikki regained her strength. In no time she was up, walking around, and talking shit. Since she's been getting washed up lately, she elected to buzz the nurse to come unhook her from the machines, so she can take a shower. When she walks past, I couldn't help but notice that Ruff Rider tattoo on that voluptuous ass of hers. I start having visions about some of the things I want to do to her. Before I knew it, I'm groping myself knowing that my soldier is the reason why this war is going on now. It just been a while since I had some, I can't help it. I limp in the bathroom and try to creep up behind Nikki in that tiny ass shower. My man got rock hard just seeing them suds run down her back to her ass crack.

"Boy what are you doing you know where we at? We can't do stuff like that in here."

"Shhhhh…I got this."

I hike her right leg up to prop her foot on the soap dish. Then I began to spread her lips and slide up her fantasy river. I take it out just to tease her a little bit, and then put it back in. I begin to stroke, and Nikki takes my hand and places 'em in her hair; wanting me to pull as I pound. As I hit it from the back her moans become louder and louder. It's so loud that the nurse that was walking past came in the room thinking she might have slip and fell in the shower. Before the nurse opens the door, she knocks and asks if everything ok. She gets no response. Then she puts her ear up to the door and realizes that's not a cry for help, that's somebody getting that twat beat! Turned on, the nurse begins to slip her finger into her warm pie. She begins tickling herself. Her passion is so high that she decides that she can't take it anymore. She opens the door but we're in the heat of the battle so we don't realize somebody is in the room. Suddenly, I feel a tongue gliding across my ass down to my nuts. The nurse runs her hands across Nikki breasts and that's where she fucked up. Nikki put the brakes on everything! She looks at the nurse with a look on her face like she has just been violated. The nurse begins to apologize saying she was caught up in the moment, and then she runs out of the bathroom.

"Nikki, why did you stop boo? We was about to be doing some "HBO Real Sex" shit in a hospital."

"I'm not with that girl on girl thing... but for you I would have tried it. That is if she would have look like something! If she didn't look like Shanaynay, we might have had action." I start laughing.

"She was kinda ugly wasn't she? My dick wouldn't even get hard for her, not ever... but we got to finish this shit here."

That's when I push her onto the hospital bed. I pinned her legs back until her body is looking like the letter "W." Her sweet potato pie is all I see. I start licking on her clit. Her Hershey kisses is running over and about to explode. She begins to go wild with ecstasy. I insert myself and give her 10 hard strokes until she couldn't hold it in anymore; then she became the Incredible Hulk. She exploded and accidently kicked the monitoring machine. It sounded off with this loud noise. The doctors came rushing as I'm scrambling to pull my pants up.

"Is everything ok in here?"

They enter the room sniffing the air. The room most definitely smells like sex.

"Yes, everything is good. I bumped into the machine by accident."

"Okay."

The doctors exit the room with this look on their face like yeah niggas we know wassup. You know I had the biggest Chuck E. Cheese smile plastered across my face. While Nikki over there not cracking a smile at all because she was embarrassed.

"These freaky ass people were in here fucking like this is The Helixx Hotel downtown some damn where..." The nurse mumbled as she left.

"Felix....Felix, wake up. You keep kicking the machine. You're making it go off." Nikki said

"Huh...what's wrong?"

I jump up and look around. Nikki's lying in the bed. Damn! You mean to tell me that was just a dream. That shit seemed so real. It's obvious that I need rest so I decided to call it a night. Hopefully, tomorrow Nikki will be getting released. We can attempt to exit the hospital again. The sunshine let us know that morning has arrived. Nikki wakes up excited that she will be leaving.

My mom is here to take her son and future daughter-n-law home. We are packing up everything, preparing for our departure. The doctor comes in for his final instructions. During the ride to Nikki's we are both acting like we haven't seen outside in forever. As we pull up, we notice a large group of people standing out front. It's a mixture of Nikki's co-workers, students, parents, and her family. They had signs, stuffed animals, and balloons. As soon as we stopped they rushed the car, with hugs, and kisses. Nikki began to cry. I think she just realized how many people she's touched. People continued to stream in all day. Eventually Nikki felt herself getting tired and wanted to lie down.

"It's time for my sister to take her medicine. Please feel free to stop past anytime but right now she needs to rest her body... so she can recover properly. Thank you so much everyone for your prayers and concern...we really appreciate it," Rashida said as she escorted them to the door.

"Baby...while you rest, I'm going to go visit Timmy and collect my mail."

"OK baby...please be careful. You know she's still out there."

"I will baby...I will."

I drive Nikki's car to the building where I once did a lot of things. As soon as I pull up a barrage of memories flood me. All types of thoughts begin to run through my head. I past a young lady walking in but all I saw was her back. *"Damn look at that walk! Shawty phat as hell!"* I say aloud. I haven't been away from Nikki for five minutes and I'm already beginning to sound like the man I once was. There's Timmy standing at the counter.

"What's up my nig…"

He catches himself.

"…Go ahead…one time and one time only you can say it."

Timmy gets so excited; like he was just inducted into the black society.

"What's up my nigga!"

I snatch him up by the collar with the look of death in my eyes. Timmy looks like he pissed in his pants. He has no idea that I'm fucking with him. I start laughing.

"Relax man…I was just playing with you. Do you have my mail? Has anybody come by looking for me?"

"Yeah as a matter of fact…the lady that just walked out the door was in here looking for you. She left her number and told me if I see you to give it to you. I think her name is Teka, Peka, Neka something like that."

"Did she say Meka dumb ass?"

"Yeah! That's her name. Babygirl is the business! She is fully loaded like a Benz with an AMG kit on it! Damn she stacked."

"I knew I seen that walk somewhere."

I dial her number and the phone begins to ring. The only problem is that Meka can't answer because she forgot her phone at the front desk. As soon as I hang the phone up Meka comes running back thru the door.

"I forgot my phone. Have you seen it?"

"That isn't all you forgot."

I extend my arms for a hug. Next thing I know, Meka slaps the shit out of me.

"I hate your black ass!"

"Where's the baby at or did you have it already?" I said looking down at her stomach.

"No you jackass…I lost the baby. I was so stressed out about my father going to jail for trying to kill his wife. He was in and out of my life but I thought at least he would be a grandfather to my baby. They said he was messing with his wife's' crack head sister. That shit was too much for me. But, the sad thing was I had to deal with that shit all alone. I didn't have you beside me when I needed you most. Do you know how much that shit hurts?"

"Baby I'm so sorry that you had to go through all of that alone. I didn't do it on purpose."

"Wait a minute….why are you walking with a cane?"

"It's a long story. I had a near death experience. It made me rethink my life. Can we go back to your place so I can fill you in on everything that's been going on?"

We both tell Timmy goodbye, grabbed some takeout and headed for Meka's house. I left Nikki's car parked. As soon as I cross Meka's door seal, Nikki begins to call my phone. I ignored the call sending her to the answering machine. I know she's going to blow my phone up so I turned the ringer off so Meka wouldn't have something smart to say. I look at the phone and see that Nikki has sent me a text message:

"You haven't been home 24 hours yet and you already back up to your old tricks. You dirty dick bitch. I pray to god you not doing what I think you doing. If so don't bother coming back ever again."

Chapter 19

I shake my head and say to myself, "*this is why I can't be in no relationship*". I love to do me! I'm sorry Lord but I might have put my foot in my mouth, maybe I'm not ready for marriage. I go and lay on Meka's bed to take a nap. She's disappeared somewhere and I'm too tired to try and figure out where she is. As soon as I laid my head down, her bathroom door swings open with the shower running.

"It's been awhile since I had some of that good dick. This new nigga doesn't do it like you! He gets off in two hours, so let's do us."

I'm in shock that she's moved on and blown that this sucker lives here. I start looking around the room but I don't see any pictures of him. Eventually, I said fuck it and hopped in the shower with her. Meka was up to her old tricks. She began to wash my body with her tongue. We get out and go to the bed. She leaves out the room and comes back with some hot tea and Halls. I'm thinking to myself that I don't have a damn cold. I lay on the bed air drying as I enjoy the hungry look in her eyes. She wants this pipe so bad it's written all over her face.

Meka takes a sip of the hot tea, then lifts my legs up a little bit, and begins blowing in my ass. This is a first for me so I don't know how to control myself. All I know is that the shit feels good. She does it again. Then she starts licking my ass with hot tea in her mouth. I'm freaking out because the shit is feeling so good. Meka pops the Hall's into her mouth and begins to give me some head. That Hall's is creating a hell of a sensation. She takes me out and starts blowing on the tip, making it tingle. Then she straddles me backwards and begins moving her body like she was hulla hooping. We were getting it in something terrible until we heard the door slam. My crippled ass hops up. Meka's trying to hide me. I get in the closet butt ass naked.

"Baby I'm hungry, horny, and tired... so you got to fix this problem."

I'm sitting here ass naked, impatiently waiting for my escape when it dawns on me that I know that damn voice.

"Anything for you honey...let me run your shower water and help take off your clothes for you."

"Naw... I'm good... is you aite Lil Mama? You acting real weird right now... like you up to something."

"Everything is cool boo why would you say that?" Meka stutters.

"If you think for one minute that I done came home from jail to be fucked over by you...you got another thing coming. Trust and believe, I have no problem with going back."

Through the closet I see him push her out of his way. He's heading to the room taking his clothes off. I'm sitting in the closet trying to find some sort of weapon but have no luck. Plus I'm ass naked, so that spells a murder in the making. I crack the closet open but can't get a good look at the guy's face. Suddenly I hear steps approaching the closet door. Oh shit! Meka runs in and slides to her knees like a baseball player stealing bases. She grabs his belongings then begins to lethal lips him. I'm in the closet watching this shit like a porno flick. She ain't never sucked my joint like that. She begins to gag on it as she does some tongue tricks. That's when he realizes he's getting the best head he has ever had in his life. The moans grow louder and he begins to coach her.

"Yes boo lick the balls... Ummm... like that... now come up a little bit.... Ummm damn girl! You making my toes curl. I need you to spit on it for me...yeah that's it. Now then slurp it up like you sucking on a straw."

"We can finish after you get out of the shower." She said after stopping abruptly.

"C'mon baby...you can't leave a nigga hanging like this."

"If you know what I know...you'd hurry up and jump in there."

"Damn! OK! Stay just like that."

He hauls ass into the bathroom and jumps into the shower. She opens the closet door and tells me to hurry up and grab my shit. I'm trying to gather up my shit and the bathroom door swings open. Meka's heart begins to race because she knows that she's as good as caught now. It's about to be some drama. The boyfriend looks at her, blows a kiss, and walks to the hall closet to get a towel. He then walks back in the bathroom.

"Shit that was a close call! Fuck this...you got to go," She whispers in a panicked tone.

My crippled ass hopped as fast as I can to the front door and makes it out. As soon as Meka closes the door, I can hear her boyfriend asking her who was at the door. She lied and said the pizza delivery man had the wrong door. Then he asked if she was going to finish what she started. Meka laughed and went to making it do what it do! I stopped listening at the door and made my way down to catch a cab back to Nikki's car. While waiting for a cab I began concocting the lie to tell Nikki. She loves me so she's going to believe it.

"Hey baby."

"Was the pussy that good you couldn't pick up the phone?"

"Man, shut the hell up with that nonsense. I wasn't fucking nobody! Why that got to be the first shit to come to your mind?"

"Yeah whatever nigga! If you weren't doing that...then what the fuck was you doing?" Nikki asks.

"I went past to see Timmy and then went to go visit Rick's mother. You know she lives in the hood...service fucked up around there."

"Ok...so I guess I'm a big dummy then huh? Because Rashida was just over by Rick mother house and she sure didn't see you or my car! So go 'head... think of a better one," Nikki says.

I look at the phone thinking damn this bitch is good!

"Girl... I was over there! What the hell I got to lie for? And how is she going to spot me anyway... by my cane? You and her can cut that BS out! Now what's for dinner?"

"Whatever you ordered... because I'm not making shit! You lying, cripple fuck!"

When I hang up a text comes through from Meka. I wonder did that nigga figure it out.

"Sex with you is always on point bad leg and all. We always have the best time around each other. I never want you to leave. Damn, I love our chemistry! Be available this week, so we can finish. P.S. I love you playboy."

I types back that I have something to tell her then my phone dies. The cab finally arrives back at the building. I jump in Nikki's car and head to her house. I need to get me a car of my own. This cab shit is played out. I just made partner so it's time to enjoy my hard work. For some reason while riding my mind drifted onto Rhonda. I wonder how she is doing? For a second I contemplated what I'd do if I saw her again. Would I give her a second chance?

I arrive at Nikki house ready to call it a night. I've just had a long exhausting day. As soon as I enter I walk straight to the kitchen to see if Nikki really cooked. She was not playing either she hasn't even boiled water in here. I look into the refrigerator to see nothing; it's bare. That's strike one! She doesn't have shit in here to eat. This icebox is bare as hell! Now I know why Nikki and her son are so damn skinny.

"Fuck," I scream out.

I go through the cabinets looking for peanut butter & jelly, Roman noodles, tuna fish, or something. Finally I find a couple packs of Ramen Noodles. I decided to whip them up. I diced an onion, threw a boiled egg in it, some Soy sauce, and a little bit of season salt. Then I made some ghetto garlic bread out of toast to go with this fake pasta dish.

"Now that's how Chef Boy-R-Dee is supposed chef up a meal."

I eat and then walk to the bedroom. I start getting ready to take a shower and get ready for bed, when Nikki comes out of nowhere.

"Let me smell your dick nigga!"

I look at Nikki with the "are you serious" face.

"Stop playing with me."

"Does it sounds like I'm playing with you nigga? Whip it out!" Nikki says

In the back of my mind I'm thinking, I got to go through this shit already this not going to work.

"Fine, here you go smell it… since you think I got something to hide. Make sure you smell every inch of this Anaconda."

Nikki begins her sniff test. She mapped her route. She started at the hairs, down to the balls, and up to the shaft. As she smells it, she is turning herself on. She grabs it and spits on it. She waits for the spit to fall off, but just before it fell, she caught it and slurped it up. That shit sent a chill up my spine. Her mouth became a vibrator and she began humming on my sack. She spits in each of her palms, puts her hands together moving them back and forth like Mr. Miagie. Her hands are hot like fire. She starts the same hand motion gently on my snake, while at the same time she was bobbing for apples. She's learned a new trick. I was trying to hold my moan in. I feel my legs going out on me. They feel like spaghetti noodles. Bam! I hit the floor. She shows me no mercy and while I'm stretched out, she's still going strong. I couldn't hold it anymore. I had to let the noises out. I'm sounding like a girl with a high pitch voice. Then she gets up grinning like she knows she just put in some work.

"I know that will bring your ass home!"

"Whooo...Lord damn! That was mean! Where the hell did you get that technique from? What sucker you been practicing with? You bet not say that you got that off TV because I watch a lot of TV and I ain't never seen that shit."

I tried to get up and take a shower but I'm too weak to walk. I'm drained. I finally get myself together, take a shower and prepare for the rest of the night. She was up watching Lifetime when I fell asleep. I slept great! I hopped out of bed and began to stretch. I yawned loudly, being funny, so that Nikki would wake up. My plan worked. She woke up with an attitude.

"I mean can you be any louder fool?" Nikki says.

"Rise and Shine! Time to give God the glory."

Nikki flips me the bird as she puts her head back under the pillow.

"You need to get your ass up so you can start planning this wedding."

"Is there any particular date and place you want it at?'

"Naw you and your folks can pick that out. Matter of fact, I'm going to call my mother to tell her come over here and lend you a hand with this stuff. I don't want you to be too overwhelmed. I don't want you to be stressed out."

I go to freshen up. I hit my mother asking her to come past Nikki's house and help out with wedding planning. I leave out with a loaded day in front of me. So many things to do, so little time! The first thing I do is text Meka. I had to let her know how much I missed her and apologize again for not being there when she needed me to be the most. She text back:

"Are you ready to finish up or you going to run? I got something for that ass."

"Listen here Babygirl… I runs from no one! Just tell me where to be and I'm on the way."

"Meet me at the Helixx at two. My last patient is at 12:30."

"Bet that! I will meet you there."

I begin to strategize my alibi. Everything has to be to the T. Every minute needs to be accounted for. I can't fumble. I want everything to line up proper. After I got my story trump tight, it was time for execution. First, I will stop past my job to surprise the Fam. I called my favorite cab driver and told him to take me to the office. While riding I decide to call home to check on Nikki. I was wondering if she went back to sleep after I left.

"What boy? You miss this that much that you couldn't wait to call me huh…is that what it is? Miss Nikki got that good…good!"

"Don't get carried away. That shit you got is alright…but don't be tooting your horn like that thing is the **Best**."

"I could've sworn you weren't saying that last night. Wasn't that you singing that Drake song, Best I Ever Had?"

"Whatever! I was only singing to take my mind off of how whack it was," I laughed.

"If you say so! But I know better than that! You were singing so you wouldn't bust so quickly."

"Ha…ha…, that shit aint funny! You know I was in an accident boo… so don't play me like that."

"Whatever punk… I will call you later so…holla."

Chapter 20

I arrive at the office ready to receive hug after hug from my co-workers. I haven't seen anyone since the incident. I looked around the office knowing that I'm lucky to have this second chance at life. The first thing I notice is the wall behind the front desk where the receptionist sits. A huge gold signs reads Law Offices of Valentine, Adams, and Williams. Immediately I was humbled and had a hard time fighting back the tears. I thought of Rick. I know he would be proud of me. I'm just standing here in amazement. I know that a lot of guys my age will never get to this point in their career. I get on the elevator to go upstairs and see the rest of the team.

Upon exiting the elevator, I hear a chorus of hand claps ahead of me. It sounds like 100 people all clapping and cheering for me as I made my way through the office. I was greeted with hugs and kisses. I took a minute to soak it all in.

"Thank you! I'm so glad that you all stood beside me through these tough times in my life. You've shown me that I do have an extended family. This means so much to me. Again, thanks to you all."

Shortly thereafter I was informed by my secretary that I've been moved to the bigger office that's across from the conference room.

"Well if you're not going, I'm not going."

"Well we won't have to worry about that. I've already moved and you have a call waiting on line 4."

"What the hell does Nikki want? I left my mother there so she wouldn't bother me…"

I go in my office and pick up the phone.

"…Nikki… what the hell you want wifey?"

"Wrong name but still your wife."

"Who the hell is this playing?"

"Your wife! The one that makes you feel good at all times."

"Toya? You crazy bitch! You've got some nerve calling me."

"Wow! I'm a bitch though? I like that. I'm glad to see you made it back to work. You're walking so well with that cane."

"What? You stalking me? I swear when I catch your crazy ass it's on! You better hope the police catch you before I do!"

"Your lil' girlfriend was lucky the first time… but just know that I don't miss twice." She laughs

"Is that a threat you loony ass trick?" I yell in the phone.

"Love you boo!" She says then blows a kiss through the phone.

This shit got me paranoid as hell. How does this crazy ass bitch always know where I am? I look at my watch and see it's time to meet Meka for our rendezvous. I tell everyone in the office good bye and that I'll be back to work real soon. I told a selected few that their wedding invitations would be in the mail really soon, so keep a look out. I can't believe that I'm finally settling down. I proceed to the elevator and out the door. But before I walk outside, I check to see if anyone looks suspicious. It looks like the coast is clear so I hop in a cab. It's only a couple of blocks over to The Helixx, so I arrive pretty quickly.

I walked to the front desk to ask them what room was Meka in. The good thing about this establishment is that you have to know the codes. The set up kind of reminds you of some Austin Powers type shit. The guy at the front desk told me which room she was in. Before going up I stopped past the bar and got a TY-KU and Goose. I through back like three of them. They are guaranteed to get the party started and make sure it lasts for a while.

I catch an elevator to the room, turned the knob, and let myself in. The room is full of white scented candles. There's a platter of fresh fruit on the bed, Rose Moet on ice, and two champagne glasses with a strawberry in each. "There's a meeting in my bedroom", is playing in the background. I walk around the room looking for Meka. I go in the bathroom where I find her sitting in a Jacuzzi full of Jello.

"Wow… I see you stepped your game up boo!"

"Take all your clothes off, then go grab those glasses of champagne and come play with me."

I follow the directions then get in the Jacuzzi with her.

"Wow…this shit is cold and gushy. This is really some different shit here! I know I'm going to be sticky as hell when I get out of here."

"Baby…that's the fun part because I get to lick it all off of you," she laughs.

We begin to talk and reminisce a little bit about who turned who out. That's when I realize that I'm not really ready for marriage. Meka is re-sparking a flame that once burned. Nikki is the furthest thing from my mind. After a while I can't take this sticky feeling. I begin to get out of the Jacuzzi so I can hop in the shower and rinse off the sticky stuff. That's when Meka stops me.

"Sit down on the edge of the Jacuzzi."

She then fills her mouth with Jello. She begins to coat my manhood with the Jello from her mouth. This shit feels some kind of good!

"Damn boo… this shit feels like I'm up in you. It's all soft, squishy, and warm. Oh my God stop! Please stop...no…don't stop," I moaned.

Then she licked my ass with some Jello on her tongue. That shit felt so good, I fell over the rails on to the floor. I hopped up so fast that you couldn't tell I was a little crippled. We cracked up laughing as we made our way to the shower to rinse the Jello off. I pick her up in the air, sat her on my shoulders and starts feasting like she had thanksgiving dinner between her thighs. When her body began to beg for me, I slid her down onto my fountain of love. She wrapped her legs around my waist and I stroked her until she started to shake like Whitney Houston when they first asked her about drugs. Meka climaxed and let off an orgasm that felt like a tsunami. The warmth of her juices excited me and let the rocket blast off into space. I came so hard that I almost dropped her by accident.

"Damn baby...that was good! I haven't felt like that in a long time."

"A long time…shit try being me. I'm living with a man that can't get up or won't touch me but every two weeks."

"Shit that couldn't be me! I would touch your ass every two minutes! What is he gay?"

"Hell if I know. He was locked up for a while so who knows," She says shrugging her shoulders.

"Well he might be a down low brother. But, fuck him! I'm here with you now…that's all that matters".

I laid her down on the bed and began to feed her fruit. Eventually, we dosed off and let the time slip by. Meka hopped up quickly once she just realized how late it had gotten.

"Oh shit! I've got to get home before this nigga start trippin'. You can stay if you want. I will text you when I get there. Shit… its eleven o clock! I got to get the fuck out of here!"

Meka rushes to puts her clothes on then gives me a kiss. She tells me that she will be glad when this sneaking shit is over. She says that she misses waking up to me. I get myself together and go check my phone. I only have one missed call from my mother. I guess it's all good. I put my clothes on and left out of the room. On the cab ride home I called my mother back to see what was wrong.

"Hello son…you was out doing something you had no business doing wasn't you boy?"

"How do you always know what I'm doing?"

"Boy I gave birth to you! I know you like a book. But that's beside the point, are you ok son?"

"Yes… I'm cool Ma. Why did you ask me that? I'm straight I guess."

"Because again… I birthed you! It's this simple… don't get married because you think that's what I want you to do. Make sure you do it because that's what your heart is telling you to do."

"I don't know what my heart is saying to do any more. At one point I thought I knew… but now I'm confused."

"Son, remember this…never confuse lust with love. Never turn in your pot of gold for a bag of trash. It will never equal out. Baby you have to let God guide you and everything will work out. I've said my peace so good night son… Mom loves you."

"I love you too Ma."

After hanging up, I thought about what she said. I start comparing every girl I've dealt with to each other. I guess I'm trying to figure out who really has what it takes to be by my side forever. When I get back to Nikki's, everyone is asleep. Nikki is sleep with wedding books, cake pictures, pictures of dresses, and flyers for locations surrounding her. I pulled the covers over her, picked up the book, and went into the living room. I sat down and started putting check marks beside the things that I liked.

I woke up with Nikki standing over me smiling. I'd fallen asleep with the books in my hand. She was very happy to see that I was interested in the wedding. The scent of food made me sit up. I hopped off the couch and walked in the kitchen where Nikki is preparing breakfast. She turns around with a big smile on her face happy that I'm really taking marriage with her serious.

"Thank you for the food that was prepared for me."

"You're welcome. What do you have planned for today?"

"I'm not sure... probably going out to get some fresh air since I was in the hospital forever. I can't stand to be cooped up in the house. As a matter of fact, I'm think I'm going to the car dealership."

"I wanna go...I want to help pick out a vehicle for you."

As Nikki walks off, I'm sitting here with the blown face. I really, really don't want her to go because I was going to probably do something I'm not supposed to. Damn! We both shower and get dressed. We drive Nikki's car up to Euro Motors in Bethesda MD. As soon as we arrive the first thing Nikki says is, "Where are the Mini Vans"? Is she serious? I'm not a minivan type dude, I'm a boss! I just made partner at a law firm! The last thing I will spend my hard earned money on is a soccer mom van. Nikki's sitting there with her lips poked out; a little offended by what I just said to her.

The salesman comes out to greet us but because we just have our throw around clothes on; he's really not checking for us. He's not showing the attention that he would show someone who looks like they have more money. I peep that off the break so I know what to do with him. Another customer just came in and they offered him water, fruit, and anything else he wanted. True enough, he had on a suit but he still didn't buy anything. I laughed to myself thinking how stupid people are. I can't believe that people still act that way this day in age. Nikki can tell that I'm a little disturbed by something.

"Is everything alright?"

"I'm good. I just hate to be treated like a bum because I treat everybody with the equal amount of respect. I ain't feeling the love right now but it's cool."

We walked around the car lot and I found the car I wanted. I told the salesmen that this is the car I would like to purchase. He looked at me like I'm speaking French.

"Are you sure that you want this car…2010 Mercedes Benz S550 with the AMG kit. You are aware that this vehicle retails for $119,000?"

"What does that mean? This is the car I said I wanted... so I suggest you do your damn job and stop pre-judging me fool."

The salesman looked at me with a stupid face. Then he wrote down the number off the car and disappeared into the sales department to do the paper work. I went through the approval process. You know the regular questions, names, job title, pay, social, etc. I tell him all of my info with an attitude. He had the "oh shit" face when I told him I was a partner in a law firm. But when that Fico score came back at 800, he almost fell out of his damn chair. That's when the ass kissing began.

"Mr. Williams is it anything I can get you and the Misses? I mean anything?"

"Yeah... you can get me your boss. I'd like to tell him how you were about to lose a valuable customer."

"I'm sorry sir. I'm sorry that you feel that way. I don't see any need to involve my boss...this was all just a big misunderstanding. I might lose my job."

"You're never supposed to judge a book by its cover. You're supposed to treat a bum on the street with the same respect that you treat the President. At the end of the day, he or she is still human."

"Yes sir…you're absolutely right. I'm sorry if I gave you that impression."

We finishes the paperwork for the title and tags and I signed on the dotted lines. When I finished they brought the car around front nice and cleaned up.

"I will meet you at the house. Then we can cruise the city…and maybe head up to Tony and Joe's to, and get something to eat by the water front."

Chapter 21

Before going to meet Nikki, you know I had stop around my old neck of the woods. I decided to visit Rick's mother. As soon as I pull up some of my buddies walked up on the car. "

"We see the recession ain't bothering you...huh playa? We know who got the money these days. We're just glad you still come and visit the poor people."

"Naw... I'm not rich. I'm blessed! Shit...a few weeks ago I almost was a memory."

"Yeah we heard about that situation...just let us know if you want us to handle that for you!"

"Yeah if ya'll take care of that for me, you know I got you."

"Bet...but what are you really doing around here?"

"I'm just dropping by to see Rick's mother."

"Man...you late. She moved right after the funeral."

"Damn! I didn't know that. Do you know where she moved to?"

"I think she moved down south somewhere."

"Good lookin' out! I'm gone but make sure ya'll handle that for me. I will be back to see ya'll."

My next stop is to go see my mother. I navigate the city bumping, *Invented Sex* by Trey Songz. All of the women are breaking their necks trying to catch a glimpse of me. I pull in front of her house and ask her to come outside.

"Wow this is a big, pretty, fancy car! How much you pay for this son?"

"I paid a nice penny for it…but do you like it?"

"Yeah… it looks like a space ship inside here with all these difficult buttons."

"You can drive it to church one day Ma."

"Oh no I won't! You will not have the church thinking I'm slanging rocks."

I begin to laugh while giving my mother a hug and kiss.

"I'm on my way to go meet Nikki so we can go out to eat."

"Bring me a doggy bag back past here."

I pull out a $100.00 bill and give it to her. Then I told her to take Sister Florence out to eat with her, my treat! I jumped in the car and pulled off headed to Nikki. I get back to Nikki's. She's in the doorway waiting impatiently. Before I can blow the horn, she's getting in. We head to get a bite to eat. When we arrive at the restaurant and we are seated quickly. We sit down and in no time flat, we are enjoying our meal. We haven't been here 15 minutes and Meka's texting me.

"I'm lonely...sitting here playing with my bullet thinking about you. You should come over tonight, my boyfriend is working a double shift. Felix my body is calling you..."

I start to think about what my mother said about love and lust. I am really starting to understand that with Meka it's more sexual. I made the right decision with Nikki so I didn't reply back. Because in my mind I know no one can come between what I got now. As soon as I look up I see Mrs. Anderson and Rhonda walking towards our table. The waiter seats them two tables away from us. Mrs. Anderson spots me and now she and Rhonda are walking over to speak. Damn! Rhonda's looking so damn good. She's shining from head to toe. She's up in that dress. It's a black fitting dress showing off her curves. She's killing me softly with these sexy ass pumps with a glass heal. Her lips are wet and shining with lip gloss. Damn! She's wearing my favorite fragrance, Envy

199

Me by Gucci. I hope Nikki doesn't see me staring. Damn, I still have feelings for her!

"Good evening Felix…how are you doing?"

"Good evening Mrs. Anderson. I'm good! Hello…how are you doing Miss Lady? When did you get out?..."

I start a conversation forgetting to introduce Nikki. That was until she kicks me under the table.

"…Nikki this is Mrs. Anderson and her little sister Rhonda. Ladies, this is my fiancée Nikki."

The ladies shakes hands and exchange compliments. I can't help but to stare at Rhonda as they walk back to their table.

"Is that the lady who won all that money that you were defending? That's the girl that Rick died over right?"

I shake my head yes. Instantly, I start reliving the times Rhonda and I shared. If that stupid shit wouldn't have went down, we could've had something special. We finish our food and prepare to leave. On the way out I stopped past Mrs. Anderson's table to give them both a hug. I gave Mrs. Anderson my new number but said it loud enough so Rhonda could hear. Once outside we strolled along the waterside. I can sense that Nikki is disturbed about something.

"Baby… is everything ok?"

"Felix please be honest with me… did you and the little sister have something going on?"

"Yeah…a good friendship baby girl! That's all! Nothing more…nothing less."

"It seems like ya'll were more than some damn friends!"

I put my arm around Nikki.

"Understand this…you're the only woman for me! Everything else is for the birds!"

We decide to go home, watch a movie, and chill with each other for the rest of the night. On the way home we stop and grab some candy, popcorn, and sodas. Once we arrived home, we changed into lounging gear and Nikki puts the movie in. I feel my phone vibrate but I try to ignore it.

"Felix….tonight I want some me time! Just you and me… without any interruptions."

"Sure baby!"

I go to turn off my phone but sneak a peek at the text message I just received. It's from Rhonda.

"I'm sorry that things didn't work out for us. I really felt like you were the one. Just know that I've learned from my mistakes. I'm happy to see you happy. She looks good with you! Big sis and I are waiting on invitations to the wedding. I love you and I'm sorry! Goodnight."

I smile as I turn the phone off. Nikki's lying on my chest watching the movie, "Brothers." It's definitely art imitating life. I feel like Shemar Moore's character. He was getting cold feet but knew that he was making the right move. I fell asleep on the couch with Nikki lying in my arms. The morning comes along and we really start getting on top of wedding arrangements. It seems like just yesterday when I asked her to marry me. Its 4 months later. These weeks have flown by fast. We have finally secured the location. We've decided on the Newton White House Mansion. The wedding will be at 4:00pm. The wedding party is ridiculous; it consist of 40 members. The invites have been mailed and we've already received over a 160 RSVP's. It's a good thing I've gone back to work because this is one expensive ass wedding. I've been spending money like a Kennedy! This wedding is top notch all the way.

Our groomsmen will take a limo bus and the bridesmaids will arrive in a Cadillac Escalade stretch limo. My mom and Nikki's parents will arrive in a pearl white Rolls Royce Phantom. Originally, I wanted Nikki to pull up in a Mercedes Benz Maybach but I switched at the last minute, and arranged for her to be escorted in a carriage pulled by a white horse. She's a queen and should be treated like the queen she is. My mission right now is to pick up my shoes. Damn! A brother can't even get some shoes without running into one of these chicks. Standing less than three feet away is none other than Meka. Meka's looking so phat! I get turned on immediately. I have to keep my composure.

"That's fucked up. You could've returned my text messages or calls."

"Meka baby…these last couple of weeks have been super busy for me. You know I just went back to work. What are you doing in the mall?"

"I'm trying to find a dress for this weekend. I'm going with my boyfriend to this wedding or anniversary… I forget what it is. But he wants me to wear a dress and shut shit down like I always do!"

"Well ok… don't let me interrupt you Boo. I'm running late to my folks. I will hit you up later."

I rushed across town to make it to the wedding rehearsal on time. I don't want to have to hear my mother or Nikki's mouth. While parking I get a phone call. I have on an ear piece so I never bother to look down at my phone.

"Hello…"

On the other end I hear someone crying.

"...Hello."

"You were serious huh! I got the invite! I don't want you to marry her... give me one more chance! Please baby...don't do this!"

I look down to see its Rhonda on the phone. I stand outside the Mansion and talk to her.

"Why did you wait three days before my wedding to start this?"

"I'm sorry ...I thought you'd see that she wasn't the one for you and that I am. Please don't make the biggest mistake of your life. You know I'm the one for you."

Now I'm stuck. I really don't know what to say.

"It's too late! The wedding is in 72 hours. I wish you would've said something earlier... but really what am I supposed to do?"

"Felix think hard about us. I mean... think about how happy we were when we were around each other. Can you honestly say that you don't love me?"

Before I can answer her, Nikki comes outside bombing me out. She says that she was just about to call me and curse me out. I guess Rhonda overhears Nikki so she hangs up. I guess she knows that I wasn't going to answer her.

"Man… don't come out here with that dumb foolishness, acting all ghetto."

"Boy…shut up! Neither you nor anybody else going to rain on my joy! This is my moment."

I walk into the mansion and begin to rehearse for the wedding. We are laughing and talking. Everyone is sharing in our moment. It's a beautiful thang if I must say so myself. The countdown begins for the wedding. It seems like the pressure is building up and the hours are moving double time. It's like every little thing is bothering me. I know that I'm about to jump into something that only the strong is cut out for. I swear that was the fastest 48 hours of my life. It's already Friday so we do all the last minute things so tomorrow can run as smooth as possible. Here we go again. Rhonda is calling.

"Hello."

"Felix…come to my sister's house and get your wedding gift because I'm not going to be able attend the wedding. My feelings for you are too strong to pretend."

"OK…I will stop past there in an hour."

I hurry and finish so that I can make my way to Mrs. Anderson's estate. I arrive and ring the door bell. I knew this was a set up. Rhonda came to the door butt ass naked! Lord give me strength. I'm trying to do the right thing but the devil is busy.

"C'mon in."

"Naw… I will wait right here until you put some clothes on."

"Boy don't act like you haven't seen me naked before. I just got out of the shower… so come on in."

My dumb ass goes in. Within 5 seconds I'm officially out of the frying pan and into the fire.

"Can you help me put lotion on my back."

"C'mon now…now you're going too far. You know that I'm getting married tomorrow."

"OK…I understand that. It's just lotion. Fuck it… she will help me."

That's when another girl comes into the room. She's naked with a body like Melyssa Ford. My mouth drops open as I watch her put lotion on Rhonda's back. They begin to kiss and their breast softly bump against each other. This shit is like watching live porn. They simultaneously make their way over to me. I feel like I'm being seduced by an octopus. I'm in heaven! They start kissing on me. Before long I am kissing them back. The friend removes my tool from the tool box and begins putting in work. Her deep throat technique has my flat head unscrewing her tonsils. I closed my eyes in pleasure and Nikki's face flashed in my head. I realize that what I'm doing is wrong, so I reluctantly push both of the women away. I zip up my pants and head for my car. My manhood is throbbing like a toothache. Damn! I should stay here and finish. I must really love Nikki to turn this down. Damn!

I drive off heading to the club where we're having my bachelor party. As soon as I enter the spot I'm greeted by all of my cousins, uncles, and friends I haven't seen in years. The first thing I notice when I walk in is the stripper lying on the floor smoking a cigarette with her pussy. A different one is atop the bar pulling a 5 foot link chain out of her woman hood. Where they do that at? This is some wild shit. Then the female that was the main attraction comes out. She lays down on the floor, open her legs, and then shoots water like 8 yards across the room, like a super soaker. Nigga what! Then she gets up and put a fire extinguisher on the ground then sat down on it. Yeah, that's what I'm talking about! The whole top of it went inside of her. This shit sent the club in an uproar. Every fella in the room is going crazy. She's still sitting on the extinguisher; another girl begins to pour hot candle wax all over her. When she asked, who was the lucky guy everyone pointed at me. She grabbed me and laid me on the ground. She ripped open my shirt and began to pour candle wax all over me. Next she licked my nipples to the point that my gun was ready to shoot. She did some type of flip and made her face end up in my crotch area. She started giving me head threw my pants.

"Shit…everyday you learn something new." I shouted.

The crowd is cheering us on. She stops right when I was about to explode. The freak show continued and the fellas continued to throw back shots. I'm feeling guilty and horny as hell so I decide to text Nikki. This is the second time today my man has been ready for war and had no competition. I just sent her a plain text asking how her night is going. She doesn't reply because she probably has some dude swinging his penis her face as we speak. Soon enough, the night comes to an end. Everyone heads home to get ready for the big day tomorrow. I guess there's no turning back now.

The morning comes faster than ever. Everybody is scrambling like a chicken with their head cut off. It's chaos at its finest. The women are starting to get there makeup and hair done. The guys are putting their tuxedos on. I remind everyone that the limos will be arriving at 2:30 sharp, so make sure they're ready. The groomsmen and I leave to go to the location where the limo will be picking us up from. We are hung-over to say the least. Just as we are getting ready to board the limo, I get a call from Mrs. Anderson.

"Felix… I have probably the best wedding gift you'll ever receive. It will be there about the same time that you arrive."

"Really…thank you so much Mrs. Anderson. You didn't have to do that."

"I wanted to…I'm very happy for you. Thanks for all that you've done for me Felix. You're a good man." Mrs. Anderson stated.

We pull up to the mansion and see another limo sitting at the top of the hill. The camera guy is snapping away. He and the videographer were instructed to capture every moment. My wedding planner greets me as soon as I step off of the limo bus.

"Who's limo is this blocking the drive way?"

"Maybe you should come and see."

We go inside and I can't believe my eyes. Standing at the altar warming up his voice by singing my favorite love song "Always and Forever," it's none other than Tyrese. I checked my swag and went and said hello to him. He said he was happy to do it and congratulated me on my upcoming nuptials. I told him to make sure he sang to the guests and not my wife and died laughing, but I was serious as a heart attack. I excused myself and walked over to the wedding planner.

"How did you get Tyrese?"

"It was a gift to you from his aunt."

I immediately texted Mrs. Anderson.

"Thank you. This was more than I expected. No words can express my gratitude.. Thank you again."

"You're welcome sweetie! You deserve it and more."

I asked the wedding planner if everything is running according to schedule. I'm anxious to get this show on the road. People are going to be talking about this wedding for years to come. I want to make sure we pull this off without a hitch.

"I have everything under control. Please head downstairs and I will come get you shortly."

Her walkie talkie goes off alerting her that our parents had arrived.

"Copy that…please make sure that you escort them to their assigned seats…"

She puts the walkie talkie back into the holster.

"…see… everything is going according to plan so relax. Let me do, what you paid me to do."

An hour goes past and the wedding is about to begin. I'm downstairs viewing everything that's taking place via closed circuit TV. I can see everything. I can see what's going outside, what guests are coming in, I see when the bridesmaids' limo pulls up, and as the planner is seating everyone. It's a packed house which makes me even more nervous. I'm nauseous as I pace back and forth. My mouth is dry like it's been packed with the cotton. The wedding planner hands me a bottle of water and tells me it's time to come upstairs.

The horse and carriage pull up alerting everyone that the ceremony is about to begin. The groomsmen and bridesmaids both line up and prepare to walk down the aisle. Tyrese begins to sing "A Ribbon in the Sky", as I walk up to the altar. Out of the side of my eye, I see Meka scream hell no and storm out crying. I played it off and took my place, waiting for my bride. The wedding party comes down the aisle, one by one. The bell girl announces that the bride is coming. Everyone turns their attention to the entrance. The doors open up and two guys with trumpets began playing the Queens arrival anthem.

There she is! MY WIFE! She's wearing a beautiful white fitted dress accented with diamond studs. Her train is so long that it reminds me of the girl from the Coming to America joint. Tyrese begins to sing, "Here and Now," and I feel myself beginning to tear up. Her father places her hands in mine. She smells so good. Diamonds blinging! She's beautiful! Right now I know that I am the luckiest man in the world! The preacher begins the ceremony and reality hits me. I begin to tear up again a little bit as I look around. I know that THIS IS IT! No turning back.

"Does anybody have any reason why these two shouldn't be joined in holy matrimony? If so please speak now or forever hold your peace..."

Rhonda jumps up with a outburst screaming, I love you and I will always love you. This shit ain't right! What the fuck just happened? Did she just do that? Mrs. Anderson grabs her and takes her outside so she wouldn't embarrass herself any further. I look at the preacher with my eyes begging him to finish this ceremony. I flash to the two potential women that could have been standing here with me: Rhonda and Meka. I remember all the shit I've gone through, from almost dying over women to breaking a lady's heart so bad that she wanted to kill me. This has been a helluva year! I was so deep in thought that I didn't hear when the preacher asked me if I take this lady's hand in marriage. I guess because I haven't answered is the reason it's so quiet in here. The preacher asked again.

"Yes...I do."

"By the power invested in me...I now pronounce you man and wife. You may now kiss your bride."

I go to lift the veil up and a thunderous crash happens from the entry doors swinging open. It's Nikki, crawling down the aisle covered in blood. I lift the veil up and damn near faint. You've got to be fucking with me! I did not just marry this crazy bitch!

PUBLICATIONS PRESENTS...

EVIL roots

BY: M. MCALL

COMING 2010

5 STAR PUBLICATIONS
www.icon5star.com
info@icon5star.com
301.568.2588

If you are an aspiring author, or already an author looking for a pubishing company you can call home and be a part of the family, 5 Star Publications is now accepting manuscripts from authors of all levels!!!

If you or someone you know are an author and looking for a bookstore to support your work of art look no further, TLJ Bookstore is the answer!!!

TLJ BOOKSTORE
www.tljbookstore.com
info@theliteraryjoint.com
301.420.1380
The Centre at Forestville
3325 Donnell Drive
Forestville, MD 20747